Sally's
Secret Legacy

OZARKS LEGACY SERIES BOOK I

AWARD WINNING AUTHOR
MARGARITE
STEVER

Publishing Coordinator – Sharon Kizziah-Holmes
Cover Design – Jaycee DeLorenzo

Paperback-Press
an imprint of A & S Publishing
Paperback Press, LLC.
Springfield, Missouri

ISBN -13: 978-1-960499-41-7

DEDICATION

To my husband, my mom, and my sister.

The three of them nursed me back to health in 2021 when I nearly succumbed to a combination of deadly maladies I had the misfortune to suffer at the same time. They dropped everything, putting their own lives on hold, to care for me. That kind of love is the truest. Without them, there would be no book.

ACKNOWLEDGEMENTS

I would like to acknowledge a few fine folks who supported me through my LONG journey of writing this book, which took me the better part of a decade.

Thanks to my husband, Jim, for giving me the space and time alone to write. Thanks to Mom who has read nearly everything I've ever written and still has most of it printed out in a binder. Thanks to my sister, Laura, who has always been in my corner, no matter my artistic doubts or meltdowns.

Thanks to my amazing friends, Tammy and Lori, who have had my back since we were kids. They have both always been willing to read my work and provide honest feedback and sage advice, whether it was what I wanted to hear or not.

Thanks to the critique partners I've had over the years. Bonnie, April, Annie, Darrell, Summer, and Claudia were not afraid to make me dig deeper, rewrite, and strive for my full potential.

Finally, thank you to my writers' groups. Joplin Writers' Guild, Ozarks Romance Authors, Ozarks Writers League, Sleuths' Ink Mystery Writers, and Missouri Writers' Guild have provided me with opportunities to learn more about my craft, pushed me out of my comfort zone, and made it possible for me to grow far more than I ever could have on my own. Most importantly, my groups allowed me to connect with other people who share my passion for words.

I would be nothing without my tribe.

CHAPTER 1

I *bet Grandpa is rolling over in his grave right now.*
Static electricity in the air tingled across Sally's skin, raising the fine hairs on her arms. She wiped away a tear as lightning forked across the sky, spotlighting the sagging old barn, which had once belonged to her grandparents.

Memories of countless hours spent with her grandfather milking cows and talking about life raced through her mind like scenes from an old movie. She had spent so much of her childhood in this old building. Its dilapidated state brought tears to her eyes. Pressing her hand to her heart to ease the ache there, she forced herself to continue, ignoring the little voice in the back of her head telling her she made a horrible mistake in coming here.

She stared at the gaping hole where the door had once been. She forced her gaze to the roof, a portion of which had collapsed onto the hayloft, causing the entire structure to tilt to the right. The once proud red building mocked her with only a few streaks of color clinging to the warped wood.

Thunder rumbled, closer this time, yanking her back to the present. She wiped away tears and hurried back to her car. She'd seek shelter in the old farmhouse until the storm passed. She thought about the tent stowed in the trunk of her car and shook her head. She couldn't possibly camp on the farm now. A tent would be little protection against the approaching storm.

The condition of the farmhouse wasn't much better than the barn, and a bone-deep weariness overwhelmed her. She should have known. The old adage, *you can't go home again,* taunted her. She'd been so excited to win the tax auction that brought her grandparents' pride and joy back to her. She'd envisioned a few repairs, some painting, and maybe a little landscaping. This was . . . she didn't even know. It was worlds beyond anything she'd anticipated.

The farmhouse roof was still in place but was riddled with various sized holes, reminding her of those kitchen sponges sold in the household cleaner aisle at the grocery store. A few green shingles fought for space with the weeds beside the house. Strips of peeling gray paint on the outside walls reminded her of happier times, and the bare wood battled rot in several spots. The old wood-frame screen door with peeling green paint hung cockeyed in place, but the actual entrance door itself was fully closed.

Sally approached the house with a heavy heart, her hand sweaty from clutching the key. She slipped the key into the lock, but it wouldn't turn. She jiggled it and shook the door, beginning to panic. Finally, the lock gave way, and she released the breath she was holding. Squeaky hinges protested as the door swung wide. Sally blinked, swallowed hard, and walked inside.

Memories of running through the door and into Grandpa's arms danced through her mind. Those sweet, happy summers filled with love, laughter, and working cattle didn't seem so long ago. She could almost smell

Grandma's freshly baked apple pie cooling on the windowsill. The fragrance of apples and cinnamon used to hang in the air so thick and sweet that you could almost taste it.

Uncle Frank had removed everything of value and then left the place to rot. That alone hurt her more than anything the old man could have ever done. There wasn't much left except the ghosts of memories past. The sunken couch drooped in the corner where her grandpa had read her stories. The bentwood rocking chair where her grandma sat and crocheted on cold nights sat in front of the fireplace, its woven seat now nothing but rotted strips.

She moved on to the kitchen and found the old yellow Formica table in the exact same spot it had always sat. Four cracked yellow vinyl chairs stood silent and dirty around the table. The wood heating stove and ancient blue washing machine faced her in silent judgment, both covered in several inches of dust and grime. A red flower pot in which her grandma had grown an African Violet sat filled with barren dirt, the plant long gone.

Sally knew there wouldn't be electricity to the house, but she'd envisioned building a fire in the fireplace for light and warmth. Searching the bin, she discovered no wood, only a few bits of bark and a couple pieces of kindling. Why had she thought there would be any? Picking up a piece of bark, she watched as it crumbled in her hand. She dusted the wood particles from her hands, feeling foolish. Nobody had lived there in years. Uncle Frank had undoubtedly burned her grandparents' wood in his own wood stove long ago.

She knew then that she must seek neighborly assistance. Mrs. Hill, her grandma's best friend and closest neighbor was the first person to come to mind. She wondered what the odds were that the lady was still alive and living in the farmhouse a couple miles away. She knew of only one way to find out.

Sally locked up her grandparents' home and hurried to her car. Driving away, she concentrated on avoiding potholes large enough to damage her car. She would deal with them later. Right now, she didn't want to be stranded miles from civilization in this storm.

Topping the mountain, she smiled at her first glimpse of the Hill house, looking just as she remembered it. The rusty cattle guard still marked the property line. The white paint looked fresh, and the windows were clean. Yellow and lavender mums lined the driveway, and pink rosebushes grew on either side of the front door, a few blooms still stubbornly hanging on despite the cooling temperatures.

Rain spattered across her windshield with increasing force, spurring her into action. It would be so easy to forget the firewood and get lost on another trip down memory lane. She had so many cherished childhood memories of this place.

Parking her car in the driveway, she sprinted to the front door. She took a deep breath and prayed that Mrs. Hill still lived there and was home. She knocked firmly on the door and stepped back so she wouldn't crowd the entrance. Visitors were not common in this neck of the woods, and she didn't want to scare the precious lady.

The door opened a crack and a silver-haired woman with cautious brown eyes peered out. After a few seconds, recognition dawned on her face, brightening her features. Mrs. Hill threw the door wide open with a big smile.

"As I live and breathe! Sally Sue Wagner, you've grown up! What brings you to my house?"

"Hello, Mrs. Hill. I bought Grandma and Grandpa's old farm. I plan to make a list of supplies and start cleaning it up this weekend. Unfortunately, this storm blew in. I didn't think to bring any firewood. Would you happen to have some that I could buy?"

"Oh Sally, my dear child! Come in, and let's get comfortable. You can wait out the storm here with us. That old house is bound to be in terrible condition. I'd be willing to bet that there are more holes in the roof than there are shingles." Mrs. Hill laughed.

"I don't want to intrude on you and Mr. Hill. I just showed up on your doorstep out of the blue. I really would love to buy some firewood if you have any extra, though."

"Mr. Hill passed away about fifteen years ago," the older woman said softly.

"Oh, I'm so sorry to hear that," Sally whispered.

"My grandson is staying here to help with harvesting. You remember Jake, don't you?"

Memories of the daring young boy who feared nothing dragging her all around the hills on his four-wheeler sprang to her mind, and she grinned. "Of course, I remember Jake. We had a lot of fun together when we were kids."

"He's in the shower right now. He just came in from the field for the day and was filthy. I'm sure you remember what hard and dirty work cutting beans is." Mrs. Hill limped to the couch, favoring her right knee. "I bet he'll be real happy to see you."

"Who will I be happy to see, Grandma?" Jake asked as he walked into the room with damp hair and bare feet. The sleeves of his red flannel shirt were rolled up to his elbows, showing his powerful forearms. His faded blue jeans hugged his muscular thighs like a koala hugging a tree.

"Sally Sue is here." Mrs. Hill beamed. "You remember her, don't you?"

The years had been kind to Jake. He was well built, a little over six feet tall with wide shoulders and muscles hewn from hard work. Laugh lines crinkled around his blue eyes, but they only added to his good looks.

"Yes, of course I remember Sally," Jake said as he strode to her with confident steps.

Sally stood and was prepared to give him a short hug when he wrapped his arms around her and lifted her in the air. Shocked, her only thought was to hold on tight.

After a long moment, Jake eased her down until her feet were back on the floor. "What the devil are you doing here after all these years, Sally?"

She took a moment to relish the scent of Irish Spring soap clinging to her skin from Jake's damp neck.

"I bought my grandparents' old farm at a tax auction. I came to start cleaning and figure out how to get it operational again. I didn't prepare for storms, so I came to ask your grandma if I could buy some wood."

She brushed a lock of shoulder length brown hair behind one ear and shook her head to hide the warmth creeping into her cheeks. "I forgot how cool autumn evenings get, especially during a storm. I don't have time to run back to town before it hits. I guess I was too excited to see the place and didn't plan very well."

Jake looked her up and down, his lips dipping in a frown. "I'm real glad to hear that you bought your grandparents' farm. But Sally, you've been in the city for a long time. It shows. I think you're in way over your head with this project."

He held a hand up to stop her when she would have argued. "That farmhouse is so far gone, I doubt you can salvage it. The barn is completely worthless and needs to be demolished. Then what are you going to do with the junk Frank left there? You'll need heavy equipment to remove some of the old machinery."

Righteous indignation consumed her. She stiffened her spine, titled her chin, and glared at him. She took a deep breath before speaking. "Jake, do I look that old and feeble to you? We are the same age. I'm in my forties, not my seventies. I will bring my farm back to life. Thanks so much for the vote of confidence." Sally snatched her purse from the couch.

"Mrs. Hill, it was wonderful seeing you again, but I need to go. I'll be sure to invite you over for a tour once everything is up and running." She hugged the older woman.

"Jake, take care of yourself." Sally flipped her hair behind her shoulder and marched to the door.

The distinct sound of someone being smacked upside the head followed her outside as she eased the door closed behind her. She couldn't suppress her tiny grin at the idea that he got what he deserved.

CHAPTER 2

L ightning forked across the sky, followed by a deafening crack of thunder as she dashed through the deluge. The nearest town didn't have a motel, but she was sure she could find one along the highway. If the weather hadn't turned so chilly, she could have set her tent up inside the old farmhouse for the night and not be forced to scramble for shelter now.

She yanked the car door open, jumped inside, and slammed it closed. Already soaked to the skin, she was fumbling with the key when Jake slid into the passenger seat beside her.

"What do you think you're doing?" Sally shouted.

"Stopping you from driving a good thirty miles to the nearest motel in a dangerous storm." Jake glared at her, his jaw set like an old Roman statue. "The roads around here flood fast, in case you forgot. You're taking me with you if you leave, so you'll have both of our lives in your hands."

"Look Jake, I'm a big girl and a capable adult. No matter what you think," she spat.

He grabbed her hand that still clutched the car keys. "Don't be flashing those gorgeous brown eyes at me. It's nice to know they're still as deadly as ever." He shook his head. "You didn't let me finish what I started to say earlier. I didn't mean you should give up and go back to the city. I meant that you can't do this on your own. You need a general contractor."

"Yes, I can. And I will. You don't know me anymore. You seem to have forgotten how tenacious I can be." She wrenched her hand from his grasp.

"I'm sure you are. You always had that stubborn streak a mile wide. I see the determination in your eyes. That doesn't change the fact that the farm will take a lot more work than you're physically capable of doing on your own, no matter how stubborn you are." Jake's voice was soft, gentle, like he was taming a skittish colt.

She closed her eyes in frustration and was startled to feel Jake's warm hand caress her cold fist. "Talk to me, Sally. Maybe I can help."

She let out a long sigh and eased back in her seat before she spoke. "I don't have a choice, Jake. I spent my life savings on that farm. I don't have the money to pay anyone to help me. Just the materials needed to begin repairs are likely to max out all of my credit cards. That's why I came here this weekend. To see what can be salvaged and what must be replaced."

She massaged her temples, trying to ease the growing ache. "I'm losing my job next spring. My company is moving its offices to New York City. It's a nice place to visit, but I don't want to move there."

"I'm sorry to hear about your job, but that's a mighty lofty goal you've set," Jake said.

She nodded. "I'm going to make a list of everything I need, then buy it a little at a time while I'm still working. I'll work on the place every weekend and holiday between now and the time I get laid off. The house needs to be habitable, so I can move in this spring. I'm going to live on my family farm, even if I'm forced to sleep in the tent I have stowed in my trunk. I plan to rent out my house in the suburbs, but it won't bring in enough money to live on."

"I see. What are your plans for the farm as a whole?" Jake's warm fingers continued to work their magic on her fist as he spoke.

She leaned her head back against the seat before she answered. "I'd like a few cattle, some chickens, and maybe some goats. I plan to contract with someone to plant corn and soybeans. I'll gladly split any profits since I don't own a tractor yet. I'm sure I can find a farmer around here willing to do that. I mean, someone has been mowing the place or the weeds would be taller than me. I thought I'd try to find out who's been doing the mowing and see if he or she would be interested."

Jake chuckled. "I've been doing the mowing down at that place for years. In return for the mowing, Frank let me harvest as much ginseng, nuts, and fruit as I wanted. He also let me deer and turkey hunt. You have a few really nice black walnut trees; in case you didn't know. Your cousin was happy with the arrangement, too. I could probably be persuaded to keep the same deal with you if it's to your liking. As for planting crops, I'm sure we could work something out."

Jake shook his head and continued, "What concerns me is the type of labor involved in repairing the farmhouse. Are you planning on crawling up on the roof and patching all those holes yourself?"

Sally slowly pulled her hand from Jake's warm grasp. "Yes, I plan on patching the roof myself. I'm sure I can get it to stop leaking at least long enough to get a good harvest, and then maybe I can have a new one put on."

The wind picked up and hailstones bounced against Sally's windshield. Jake looked at her and said, "You're staying here with us until the storm passes, and we need to get inside now."

"Yeah, okay," she sighed.

They dashed into the house to find Mrs. Hill standing just inside the door, hands on her hips with one foot tapping the entryway tile.

"Took you two long enough," she snapped.

"Sorry, Grandma. Sally and I had a lot to talk about."

Mrs. Hill walked to the coffee table, grabbed two neatly folded towels that she'd apparently gathered earlier, and tossed them to Jake.

"Dry yourselves off. You're dripping all over my floor." Mrs. Hill continued, sounding like a true grandmother, "I have milk and cookies for you in the kitchen."

Jake handed Sally a towel, and they dried off before following the older woman into her warm kitchen. She'd been expecting cookies from a package, but she should have known better. A plate piled high with home-made chocolate chip, sugar, and peanut butter cookies sat proudly in the middle of the kitchen table. Three plates, three glasses, and three napkins were arranged on the crisp white tablecloth next to a pitcher of fresh milk.

Overcome by emotion, Sally swallowed the lump in her throat at the memory of her grandmother preparing the same snack for her when she was little. At that moment, she knew that buying the farm was the right thing to do. She belonged in the fresh air with the clean water and the bullfrogs singing her to sleep. She belonged with kind country people like these. She smiled and hugged Mrs. Hill tightly.

"Thank you so much. You have no idea how you've touched my heart tonight." She wiped a stray tear from her cheek.

Mrs. Hill returned her hug with a strength that belied her advanced years. "Welcome home, Sally Sue. I always thought your family home place was where you belonged."

"Thank you. You were so kind to me." She let out a soft

chuckle. "Some of my earliest memories are of Grandma and you taking me to pick blackberries and teaching me about self-sufficiency. I never forgot those lessons."

The older woman patted her hand. "Take a seat, honey. Have some cookies and milk. We have a great many years of catching up to do." Mrs. Hill claimed a seat and began filling her plate while Jake poured the milk. "So, tell us what you've been doing since you were twelve or so."

Sally snorted. "Well, I don't think you really want to go back quite that far. Maybe I should start with the present. I work for an advertising agency. I've been with them for ten years. The work is challenging and fast-paced. I like my job, but not enough to move to New York City to keep it."

"So, do you plan on working the farm then?" Mrs. Hill asked.

"Yes. I don't enjoy being in the city anymore. It's never quiet. I'm tired of dealing with the noise and traffic. Even in my subdivision, it's never quiet. I've been to bigger cities a few times for business meetings, and I certainly don't want to move to any of them. I'd never have any peace at all."

She took a deep breath and continued. "When my boss announced that our agency would be relocating, I told him I wouldn't be going. That's when I started looking for a small place in the country. I really haven't been happy for a long time. Imagine my surprise when I found Grandma and Grandpa's place listed."

Mrs. Hill nodded, her wisdom obvious in her every move. "Some folks just have country in their veins. You always have. Your grandma used to worry herself sick about you being in the city around all the drugs and violence."

"I've survived well enough. My location didn't really bother me until recently. There's just something inside me that wants to live in the fresh air, grow my own food, and do my own thing without my neighbors being able to see everything I do," Sally said.

She studied her empty milk glass for a moment. "That's enough about me. So, Jake, tell me what you've been up to."

"Well, I own a construction business in Columbus, and I do general contracting, as well." He shifted in his seat, stretching his long legs out in front of him. "I have really good people, so I can take time off to help Grandma without worrying about my company going belly up while I'm gone. I usually spend my weekends and holidays here or on some other farm helping out in one way or another."

"So, you don't have a spread, yourself? I always pictured you getting up at the crack of dawn to milk cows and work your own place."

"I have a few acres about fifty miles from here. I plant corn, but that's about it. I don't have any livestock to take care of, so I don't need to be there all the time," Jake explained.

"So, when the time comes, maybe I can have your company replace my roof. Would you mind giving me an estimate?"

"I'll be happy to give you an estimate when you're ready. It wouldn't do any good to do it now because material prices fluctuate all the time."

Mrs. Hill's eyes gleamed with mischief as she added to the conversation. "Jake was married to Mary Southern for about five years, but it didn't work out. They didn't have any kids, so there's nothing to tie him to his house. It's not really a home. It's just a place for him to sleep and eat an occasional meal."

Jake gave Mrs. Hill a warning look. "Grandma, do you have a point?"

"Sally, are you married, or have you ever been?" she asked, ignoring Jake's question.

"I was married for a couple of years to a guy I met right after college. I'm divorced now. We had different philosophies about life. I thought that we should both have jobs, and he had the idea that he should sit home on the couch playing video games while I supported him." Sally shook her head. "I don't mind doing my share, but I don't need any dead weight."

Jake looked thoughtful for a moment and then asked, "Is your last name still Wagner or something different?"

"I did take his last name while we were married but reclaimed my own when we divorced. We didn't have any kids, so there was no point in keeping it. I certainly didn't want a reminder of my biggest mistake for the rest of my life."

They talked well into the night while the storm raged outside. They ate all of Mrs. Hill's cookies and drank the pitcher of milk while the power blinked on and off. At one point in the evening, their loving host served sandwiches and iced tea for a quick dinner.

Mrs. Hill stood up around midnight and announced it was bedtime. She insisted that Sally spend the night in the spare room and instructed Jake to retrieve her suitcase from the car. Sally protested when Jake grabbed her keys and bolted outside. He was back a moment later, dripping wet with her suitcase in hand. He shook himself like a dog, water droplets spraying everywhere.

"Thank you." Sally reached out to take the suitcase from him.

"This thing weighs a ton. I'll carry it up to the spare room. It's right next to my room, so don't even give me any sass over it."

"Okay. Thanks." She tried to keep the quiver from her voice.

They climbed the narrow wooden staircase in silence. Jake put her suitcase down just inside the guest room, showed her the upstairs bathroom, and where to find the towels. Then he seemed at a sudden loss for words and simply stared at her for a moment.

"If you need anything, I'm right next door." He pointed in the direction of the bedroom he was using. "I'm a light sleeper, so I'll hear if you knock."

"Thanks. I can't think of what I would need, though." She looked around and tried to fight the blush she could feel creeping up her neck.

"Sally, I'm really glad you forgot to pack the wood and the storm came through," Jake said softly as he slid his arms around her for a sweet hug. "Good night."

"Good night, Jake. Thank you for everything. You and your grandma are life savers."

"Just out of curiosity, where would you have gone if I hadn't stopped you?"

She shrugged. "I was going to get on the highway and drive until I found a motel."

"An attractive woman like you doesn't ever need to be staying in one of the fleabag motels by the highway. They find meth labs in those all the time, you know."

Sally laughed. "I live in the city. The police are always finding meth labs, hookers, dead bodies, and illegal weapons in our motels."

"Oh, Sally." Jake hugged her again. This time, he didn't let go for a long while. She could feel his heartbeat against her cheek and wondered if he planned to hold her all night. A part of her she didn't want to examine wished he would.

"Goodnight, Sally," Jake whispered in her ear just before releasing her.

"Goodnight, Jake," Sally said softly.

When he left, closing the door with a soft click, Sally gathered her toiletries and headed to the bathroom. After taking care of her nightly ritual, she tiptoed back to her room. As she passed by his door, she could hear him snoring like a lumberjack. She smiled. The poor guy had to be exhausted. He most likely got up with the chickens every morning and worked hard all day. Then she came along and kept him up half the night.

She changed into her pajamas and slipped into bed. Lying there, waiting for sleep to claim her, she wondered what it would be like to drift off to sleep cuddled up next to Jake on a night such as this. She imagined he would keep a woman nice and warm.

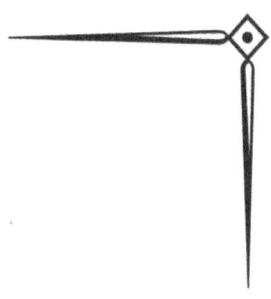

CHAPTER 3

Waking to the aroma of biscuits permeating the air, Sally rolled out of bed and stumbled to the bathroom to brush her teeth and take a quick shower. When she emerged, the scent of bacon and eggs intermingled with the biscuits. Her knees nearly buckled at the homey smells.

She packed her bag and hurried down to the kitchen where she found Mrs. Hill and Jake sitting at the table. Piled high in front of them were the bacon, eggs, and the biscuits that had smelled so good. Home-made jam in three different flavors beckoned her. She could practically hear the angels singing as her gaze caught on the lone crock of what she would bet her last dollar was home-made butter.

"Good morning," she greeted her hosts.

"Good morning, Sally Sue," Mrs. Hill responded with a smile. "How did you sleep?"

"Like a rock. Thank you."

Jake offered her a sleepy smile. "Grandma made a light breakfast. The bacon is crispy, the eggs runny, and the biscuits fluffy. Join us."

"Thanks. I'm starving." She plopped down in a chair and filled her plate.

They ate in silence, and she could not remember starting a day feeling so good. This was further proof that country living was for her, no matter the doubts she'd suffered the night before.

After breakfast Jake took off for the field, and Sally thanked Mrs. Hill before leaving for her own farm. The storm had left the ground muddy and the air fresh, whispering to her of new beginnings. Water droplets clung to each blade of grass making the world look a little magical. She could almost believe in magic on a morning such as this, but she'd learned better long ago.

She drove to the house to start her list since a place to live was her top priority. The barn would be her second priority. She still struggled with the front door lock, but it was a bit easier than last time. She made a mental note to get some WD-40 to loosen up the lock. This time when she walked through the door, she concentrated on what would be instead of what had been.

She knew Grandpa always kept things around to use for repairs, so the first order of business was to see if there was any usable material left. After opening several drawers in the kitchen, she found her grandparents' ancient silverware and some odds and ends. She finally found the junk drawer and nearly jumped for joy. Uncle Frank didn't care about the mundane everyday stuff, so it only made sense that he left all of the junk.

She dug through the drawer with reverence, separating solidified rubber bands from handy things such as screw drivers and thumb tacks. At last, she found that for which she'd been searching. Tucked into an old bread sack in the back of the drawer was a collection of tin can lids. Joy filled her heart as she spread them out in front of her. Her grandpa had once told her these made great hole patches.

She'd even watched him nail one to the floor of the barn to cover a mouse hole.

"It's a temporary fix, Sally," he had said, "but it will get you by for a while."

Getting by was exactly what she needed to do. The bread sack contained several dozen lids, so she might have enough to cover all of the holes in the roof. It was a good start. She set the bread sack on the table next to the screw drivers and thumb tacks. Continuing her search of the kitchen, she found Grandma's old cast iron skillet and put it on the table next to the tools she'd pulled from the drawer.

She walked through the house making lists of things that she could keep, things she needed, and things to pitch. Sally grabbed her additional supplies from her car, swept, cleaned out the remaining drawers and went in search of a ladder. Inside the tool shed, where an old steam engine belt hung on one wall, she found the ladder she'd hoped for and stuffed some nails in her pocket. She examined the ladder, then tested it by bouncing her weight on the bottom rung. With a shrug and a prayer, she hauled it out, anxious to begin the real work.

She tied the bag of lids to her belt loop, grabbed her hammer, and carefully ascended the ladder. She paused at the top to examine the roof. She didn't see any rot or obvious bowing, but that didn't mean it was safe. She carefully put one foot on the roof and eased her weight onto it. When it held, she put her other foot on the roof, making her way to the first hole. Pulling out a nail and a tin lid, she patched the hole. When it held, she felt like she had the world by the tail.

Being nobody's fool, she made her way over the roof with great caution. She'd patched eight or nine holes with the tin lids when she heard gravel crunching on the driveway. Since she wasn't expecting anyone, she ducked close to the shingles until she could see who was coming.

A big blue Chevy pickup pulled up the driveway and

parked next to her car. She raised up to the sight of Jake throwing open the truck door and staring right at her. He propped his hands on his hips and slid his aviator sunglasses down his nose. His eyes were spitting fire so fierce, she could feel the heat even on the roof.

"Sally, what the hell are you doing up there?" Jake's glare would have wilted a weaker soul.

"Patching the holes." She shook her head in an effort to clear it. "What are you doing here?"

"Grandma made you some supper, and I thought I'd be neighborly and deliver it. I just didn't expect to find you doing something so dumb. Come down here before you kill yourself."

"Hey, I've been working really hard here," she answered in the same loud tone. "And it's not dumb to patch a leaky roof!"

"Sally, please come down." Jake held the bottom of the ladder. "I have fried chicken with all the fixin's, and I even brought some fresh lemonade."

Her stomach rumbled at the sound of food. "Okay, I'm coming down. Hey, what do you mean she made supper? It can't be that late."

"It's almost five o'clock."

"Oh." She rubbed her nose. "I missed lunch. Must've lost track of time. I made some great headway, though."

When her feet were firmly on the ground, Jake grabbed her by the shoulders, and whispered, "Stay off the damned roof. I don't want you killing yourself."

"Those holes won't patch themselves."

"You can hire someone to do that for you. A professional."

Her spine went as stiff as a redwood. "Stop treating me like I'm a toddler who wandered away from her mama. I'm a grown woman and make my own decisions."

"Okay, you're right. I'm sorry." He took a deep breath before speaking again. "So, what are you using for patches?"

Untying the sack of lids from her belt loop, she handed them to him.

Jake chuckled. "I see you listened to your grandpa's stories. I remember how he told us the old timers used these, but there are better ways."

"Well, these were handy, so I'm using them." She folded her arms over her chest and cocked her hip.

He shook his head and started up the ladder.

"Hey, what do you think you're doing?" She could feel her blood pressure rise.

"Checking your work. You know, I do this for a living," Jake snapped.

He surveyed her work and nodded. Grinning, he descended the ladder.

"Okay Sweetness, I see that you've worked hard. Your methods may be unconventional by modern standards, but with a little tar to seal them, they might just stop the leaks. Not bad. Time for supper." He flashed her a sexy grin before he turned and walked to the truck. He returned with a large picnic basket.

She led the way into the kitchen. "I'm sorry, but I don't have any utilities yet. We have to wash up with baby wipes."

Jake set the basket down on the old kitchen table and cleaned his hands with a baby wipe. Reaching into the basket, he pulled out plates, napkins, silverware, a thermos, and several bright orange containers with perfectly sealed pleated lids.

Sally wiped her hands and face while Jake set out the food. When he opened the first container, her knees went weak at the scent of Mrs. Hill's fried chicken. They ate in silence and with gusto. When they were finished, she sat back with a sigh of contentment.

"Your grandma still knows her way around a chicken." Sally licked her fingers.

"Yeah, she does. I don't go hungry at her house. That's for sure."

He studied her for a moment, his eyes earnest and serious before asking, "Sally, where are your mom and dad?"

"They retired and decided to go to Africa on mission work."

"Do they know you bought this place?"

"No. I'll write to them and tell them after I'm settled in," Sally answered. "While I can't reach them directly, there's a Post Office box I can mail things to. They check it every few months. Why?"

"I was just thinking about how your dad would react to seeing the farm as it is now."

"Well, he won't see it until it's up and running again, so there's no need for you to worry."

Jake nodded, deep in thought as he stared off in the distance.

"Thanks for coming by and bringing supper, but I need to get some wood cut before dark. I'm losing light." Sally stood and stacked the containers in the picnic basket.

"Did you bring a chainsaw?"

"No, but I have an ax that I found in the tool shed. I'm just going to pick up dead wood on the ground and use the ax to chop it to size."

"Let me help you. I know where there are some trees down. We can take my truck. It'll hold more than your car," Jake offered.

"Thank you, but I don't want you to feel like you need to help me just because we were childhood friends. You must be tired from working all day. You should go back to your grandma's and get some rest. I appreciate everything you've done."

Jake caught her arm as she started to turn away. "I want to help you cut the wood. I'll sleep a whole lot better if you let me help you."

"I have to admit that I'm starting to feel muscles that normally don't get used, so I'll gladly accept your offer. Thank you."

She started to lift her ax from the corner where she'd propped it when he said "I have my chainsaw, so we should be able to make short work of this."

"That sounds like a better idea than mine." Sally said.

She climbed into the truck and leaned back into the supple leather seat, staring out the window as he drove with care up the steep slope of the hill. Reaching the top, her heart cried for what had been. The pastures that once held cattle and goats were overgrown with crabgrass and weeds.

"I remember coming up here with Grandpa to round up the cows for shots," Sally said with a quiver in her voice. "Now the pastures just look wrong. Did Uncle Frank take all of the livestock or did he sell them?"

"He sold the cows and goats at the livestock auction and then had a big auction here and sold all of the equipment. He sold some of the antiques, but kept most of them. I guess your cousin, Danny, probably inherited them."

"I wouldn't know," she whispered.

They fell silent. The only sounds were the rushing water and the crunch of truck tires on creek gravel as they crossed a shallow stream. Watching the water splash up on her door, she was overcome by memories of being thrilled to take this exact path with Grandpa while he did his chores.

"Why are there so many dead trees? What happened?"

"We've had several ice storms since your grandparents lived here. I removed the ones that fell across the main pasture areas, but Frank told me to leave the ones in the woods. Several of these are well seasoned, so they'll burn without a problem. Have you checked to be sure your chimney is clear?"

"No. I hadn't thought about that. I should look before I build a fire. There are probably bird nests and who knows what else in there after all this time."

"We can check it when we get back to the house. I still think you should stay with Grandma again tonight, though."

"I can handle staying by myself. Although the fact you have a chainsaw makes me really happy that you stopped by." She grinned.

They cut and loaded enough wood for the weekend and headed back downhill. Jake was careful to avoid the large limestone rocks along the rutted trail. They took their time, not wanting any wood to fall out of the truck.

Back at the house, he climbed up on the roof and shined a flashlight down the chimney while Sally looked up from the fireplace. There was a little debris to be removed, and they cleared it with no problems. It wasn't cold yet, but the chill would be on them soon.

They made short work of stacking the wood next to the hearth and laying the fire. Sally laughed with glee as the flame caught the seasoned wood in a beautiful dancing blue and red blaze. Jake put his arm around her shoulders and the two of them stared into the fire, transfixed by the merry flames.

"Sally, where do you plan to sleep tonight?"

"I'm going to spread my sleeping bag out in front of the fire and sleep here in the living room."

"What about varmints? What will you do if a raccoon decides to join you?" His nostrils flared with a deep breath, and he pulled her further into the shelter of his body.

Sally laughed. "Since raccoons tend to be vicious little buggers, I will hold real still until he gets bored and goes away."

"What about . . ." he began, but she cut him off.

"This is my grandparents' house. It was left to rot for years, but I am back to save it now. It's rough, but I feel safe here. I'll lock the doors and be just fine."

The big man shook his head. Still not looking convinced, he turned her to fully face him and peered deeply into her eyes.

"Look," she said, "you are not responsible for me. I'm an adult. I have survived without you for a few decades. I didn't suddenly become helpless and weak just because I ran into you now." She propped her hands on her hips and stared him down.

Huffing out a breath, he looked deep into her eyes. "It seems everything I say offends you in some way. I'm sorry for that. I know that you're capable, and you certainly aren't a fool. Is it such a bad thing that I care what happens to you?"

"No, Jake. It isn't a bad thing that you care what happens to me at all. I'm glad you do. I missed you over the years. I really did."

"Come back to Grandma's with me tonight. Please. You have no electricity or running water." He looked around with a snarl twisting his lips. "There are still holes in the roof, and you have no idea what might be hiding in the dark corners and crannies of this house."

"I need to stay here. This is my home. Well, it's the only place I've ever felt at home, anyway. I have some oil lamps, a nice snug sleeping bag, and firewood. I've checked the whole house and found no varmints. I will be fine."

"Then let me stay here with you." He rested his hands on her shoulders.

"No, I need to do this by myself. Please try to understand. This is personal for me. Besides, your grandma has already been way more than kind. I don't want to impose on her good will."

"She'd feel a lot better if you came back to her house with me. You don't have to worry about me sneaking into your room if that's what's stopping you."

Sally snorted. "Wow. You have a high opinion of yourself. I'm not worried about you sneaking into my room. I'm staying here because this is a homecoming for me. I need to stay here tonight. I can't explain it any better than that."

Jake's breath whooshed out as he nodded. "I can't fault you for that. Does your cell phone have enough of a charge to last the night?"

She checked her phone. "I have 75%, so it should last until tomorrow afternoon."

"I need you to take my number and give me yours. If something happens, even if you just feel scared, I want you to call me." The intensity of his gaze brooked no argument.

After they programmed their numbers into each other's phones, he enfolded her in his arms for a sweet hug. Pulling away, he studied her for a moment. "I need to get back to the house. You take care tonight. And for the love of God, call me if you need anything."

"I'll take care. I promise. I'll call you if I run into any trouble. Now, get back to your grandma's, so you can catch some shut-eye. I'm sure she expects you at church in the morning." She flashed a knowing smile.

"That she does. It won't be long before she'll start insisting that you join us, too. She'll probably wait until you at least have electricity, though," Jake laughed.

Hugging him one more time, she whispered, "Thank you for everything."

He nodded, kissed her forehead, and left.

She watched his taillights fade into the distance with a slight fluttering in her tummy. She couldn't shake the feeling that she may have gotten more than she bargained for when she knocked on Mrs. Hill's door.

Sally spent a few more hours cleaning and securing the place. Piecing together a broken window pane as if it were a puzzle, she took great care in taping the cracks. She cleaned the kitchen table and counters using the all-purpose cleaner she'd brought with her. As she cleaned the sink and appliances, she wondered if any of them still worked.

Glancing at her watch, she was shocked to see that it

was nearly 9 o'clock. She'd cleaned a great deal by firelight. She spread her sleeping bag on the freshly swept floor in front of the fireplace, wiped herself down with baby wipes, and climbed into the coziness of her new flannel-lined deluxe camp bag. She'd spent a small fortune on the thing, but she realized it was worth every penny the moment her feet touched the soft warmth. Surrounded by the comforting scents of wood smoke and baby wipes, she drifted off to sleep.

CHAPTER 4

E arly the next morning, the aroma of fresh baked apple pie pulled her from her dreams. She looked around in confusion for a moment.

"Jake? Are you here? Did your grandma bake apple pie? Jake?" She looked around, but there was no sign of him. She searched the kitchen and living room, but found no pie.

Boy, I must be more tired than I thought. I'm hallucinating the smell of pie.

As she prepared for the day, the smell of pie hung in the air, but she decided it was just wishful thinking. She made a mental note to stop by a bakery on the way home.

She set about her various tasks in her endeavor to make the house habitable. She was busy measuring the rotten boards on the exterior of the house when Jake pulled up. Surprised, she could see that he had a young man with him.

"Hi, Sally." Jake climbed from the truck and gestured to the teen who came to stand by his side. "This is Chase Crawford. He goes to Grandma's church. He's been looking to break into the carpentry field, but needs some experience."

"It's a pleasure to meet you, Chase. I'm sure carpentry is a great field." She accepted the hand the teen offered in a firm grasp.

"It's nice to meet you, too, ma'am," he said with a shy smile.

"We got to talking at church about your project here, and I had an idea. Chase needs a good reference in order to get a decent job when he graduates from high school. You need someone to make a lot of repairs around here."

"Yes, that's true. So, what's your idea, exactly?" Sally asked.

"Well, he can work on things around here between school and his job at the local grocery store. He gains experience and a reference, and you get work done throughout the week when you can't be here. The kid is handy as can be. You give him a list, buy the material he needs, and he won't let you down."

"Miss Sally, I wouldn't charge you anything for labor. I just can't get a carpentry job around here without experience because everybody knows my dad's in jail. They think that just because he's a good-for-nothing, I am too. I'm not my dad. I'm a good worker. I'm honest, too. Please don't judge me by my dad," Chase pleaded.

Studying the young man, she tried to form her answer. He looked to be nearly six feet tall with a lean runner's build. A good-looking young man with black hair and guileless brown eyes. He looked to be about sixteen or so. "I can't pay you anything. I don't feel right about you working for free." She shook her head.

"Miss Sally, I'm in need of a good reference. If you let me work for you and tell any prospective employers what a good and honest worker I am, then my chances of getting a good job after high school will be much better. We'd be helping each other."

"Sally, could I talk to you privately for a minute,

please?" Jake asked.

"Sure." She led the way into the house.

"He's a good kid. He just needs a little help. It's not his fault that his dad's in jail. Surely, you wouldn't hold that against the boy?"

"No. I don't hold that against him. You can't judge a person by his or her family. What did his dad do, anyway?"

"He had a bad drinking problem. One night he beat up Chase's mom and then went out and robbed a liquor store at knifepoint. It didn't take the police long to catch up with him. He went right back home where the boy's mom had up and left. No one has heard from her since." He shook his head. "Thankfully, Chase wasn't there that night. He was spending the night with a friend. He lives with his aunt now. You probably remember her. She went to Sunday school with us. Christy Sims. Well, her married name is Jones. She's a distant cousin of mine. I think she's a year or so older than you," Jake said.

"I do remember Christy. She was nice. So, Chase's mom would be her little sister, Pam, then?"

"Yeah, it's been six years and no one has heard a word from her. The common thought around town is she probably hopped a bus and got as far from here as she could. If she actually did that, I don't understand why she left her son."

"Oh, that's just terrible." Sally put her hand to her chest, imagining the boy's pain.

"So, will you help the kid?" Jake asked. "You help him, and he helps you. I've seen him work around Christy's place and the church. The kid's got some skill. You could have him replace those rotten boards around the base of the house, cut more wood for the fireplace, replace the broken glass in the window, and whatever else needs done. Wouldn't it be nice to have some of this stuff being done throughout the week?"

"It would, but I don't feel right about him working for

free."

"He wouldn't be working for free. He'd be working for a good reputation and some pride. Think of it as an internship. He's shunned almost everywhere he goes. That's the problem with these small farming communities. Everyone knows everyone and all of everyone's business. He only got the job at the grocery store because Grandma beat the manager in a card game. If he won, Grandma had to supply his bakery with cookies. If she won, he had to hire Chase."

"Okay, I'll go talk to him. Maybe I can add something to my end of that trade to make it fairer for him. If I can make the farm profitable, perhaps I could chip in for him to further his education after high school. He strikes me as a trade school kind of guy."

When they went back outside, Chase was leaning against the porch railing looking like he had lost his last friend. He straightened at their approach.

"Miss Sally, I'm sorry we put you on the spot like that. I understand if you want nothing to do with me. I'll just head to the truck now." Chase turned to go with his shoulders slumped.

"Wait," she hollered. "I have no objection to you helping out around here. My objection is to you working for free. I can't pay you, but perhaps there is something else that I could trade for your carpentry services."

"Honestly, Miss Sally, there is something that I would really like if you insist that just giving me a good word isn't payment enough." His eyes brightened as he spoke.

"What is that?"

"Peanut butter cookies. My cousin is allergic to peanuts, so we don't ever get to have anything with peanut butter in it. I sure do love them, though. I think my labor for a batch of peanut butter cookies every week would be a right fine trade," he said with a grin.

"I can handle that. I deeply appreciate your help and

look forward to working with you." She extended her hand to seal the deal with a handshake.

The teen's grip was warm and firm. "Great! So, where do I start?"

"Well, I really don't have much material here right now. I'll make a list for you and bring more supplies next weekend. I'll also bring a batch of peanut butter cookies for you."

"I can start right now. I know you're trying to get the house fixed up so you can live in it. Jake said you have a time limit on that." He rubbed his hands together as he looked around.

"Sally," Jake began, "did you finish patching those holes on the roof yet?"

"No. I was just about to climb up there and get going."

"Chase, I'll get you started on that while Sally makes a list of other things that need done. I brought some roofing tar with me, so we can get those holes sealed up before the next rain comes in a few days."

"Yes, sir! Thank you kindly for this opportunity, Miss Sally." The boy's cheeks reddened as he turned away.

She went inside to get her list of repairs, can lids, hammer, and nails while Jake grabbed the roofing tar from his truck. They met by the ladder where Jake instructed Chase on the repairs. Sally handed the supplies over to the youth and watched as he scaled the ladder like a monkey.

CHAPTER 5

"I still feel like I'm taking advantage of the boy." She rubbed the bridge of her nose.

"You're helping him more than you can imagine. Christy has done her best with him, but she has kids of her own to take care of. It doesn't help that her husband hates him. Just treating him like a regular person will do wonders for his self-respect. Baking him cookies will make him feel real special. He'll do a good job. You'll see."

"Well, thanks for bringing him with you. He'll move my time table along nicely if he can work a few hours during the week."

"Now, let's take a look at that list of yours. I might have some of the material up at Grandma's house like I did the tar. I keep a few supplies there because sometimes I head to a job site from her house instead of going home first. She doesn't seem to mind, and it sure saves me gas," Jake said.

Sally handed him her list of repairs and supplies. He looked it over and nodded. "I have some lumber at

Grandma's house that would work for the rotten window frames. I should also have some sealant that we can use to keep the wood from aging."

"How much lumber do you have? If you have enough for the window frames, then I'll pick up enough to replace the exterior boards." She tapped her chin. "After those are replaced, I can think about painting. That will help preserve the house."

"You really need to think about getting some sort of siding. Painting it is all well and good, but vinyl siding will last for decades," Jake said.

"You're thinking like a contractor now." She sighed. "I don't have the budget for siding at the moment. Maybe after I'm here for a few years and the farm is making some money, I can think about such things. Right now, I need to get by until I have a harvest or two and funds aren't so tight."

"I'm going to try to help you stretch your budget. I have a few odds and ends left over from various jobs that you can have. I make enough money on my jobs to cover it. I just don't like to waste anything, so if it's still good, I refuse to pitch it," Jake smiled.

"Thank you for all of your help." She wiped a stray tear from her eye.

"It's my pleasure to help you make this place prosperous again. Grandma and I were sick at the idea of this fertile land just sitting here rotting away. I have faith that you'll make this work," Jake said.

Sally looked up at her old childhood friend who had become such a handsome man. He was still a loving and generous person just like he had been as a kid. Lost in those thoughts, she felt his arms come around her in a warm embrace. She snuggled into him for a moment and enjoyed the feel of his strong arms around her.

"I'm going to head back to Grandma's house and see what I have there. I'll be back later with whatever supplies

I can gather. Then we'll get Chase lined out for the week and make your supply list. Sound like a deal?"

"Yeah, but don't you have more beans to cut?"

"No, I finished yesterday. Today I'm all yours," he said with an intense look in his eyes. "If you want me, that is."

He leaned in and kissed her forehead. He was halfway to his truck before Sally recovered from his simple kiss to her forehead.

Good Lord, what would I do if he actually kissed my mouth? I'd probably have a good old-fashioned swoon!

She resumed her measurements of boards that needed replaced and made the appropriate notes. Then she walked back to the pump house to see if she could see any damage there. She was wondering about the cost of having a professional look at her pump when she heard a noise behind her.

She whirled around and let out a surprised yelp when she saw Chase standing in the doorway blocking the sun.

"I'm sorry to startle you, Miss Sally," he said. "I'm finished with the roof. Do you want to take a look at it and make sure I didn't miss anything?"

"Sure. Sounds like a plan." She felt her heart slow back to normal speed.

Climbing the ladder to the roof, she surveyed Chase's work. It looked like he'd done a good job. There were tarred can tops covering all of the holes that she could see. The roof looked pretty solid. She turned to descend the ladder and was once again startled to see the kid right behind her.

She squeaked, losing her footing. He had her by the arm and was helping her regain her balance before she could even blink.

"Careful there, Miss Sally," the boy crooned. "I don't want anything happening to such a nice lady as you."

"Thanks," she breathed. "You're a life saver. You have ninja reflexes. Falling off the roof is not on my list of things to do today."

"Well, as long as I'm around, I won't let you fall. Does the roof look okay? Did I miss any spots?"

"Looks good to me," she said peering at the repairs again. "I think it'll look even better from the ground, though."

Chase climbed down first and raised his arms to catch her in case she slipped. The boy was really sweet, even if he was too quiet.

Once her feet were planted on solid ground again, she took him around the house and pointed out the boards that needed replaced.

"Jake said he thinks he has lumber and sealant at Mrs. Hill's house, so you should be able to start on some of it this week if you want." She touched his arm. "You really only want a batch of cookies for all of this work?"

"Yes, ma'am. Just being somewhere quiet like this and knowing someone is going to give me a good reference is all the payment I need. The cookies are just a bonus." A slow smile spread across the boy's face.

The sound of a vehicle made them both look up to see Jake coming down the driveway. He parked his truck and got out to unload the lumber. Chase rushed to help him.

"We have enough lumber here to replace all of the decayed window frames and some of the boards on the exterior walls. We'll start with the worst boards first. I'll show you how I'd like to have it done. Sally, you can follow behind us with the wood sealant if that works for you," Jake said. "Once we get a section replaced, you paint the sealant on with a paint brush."

"Okay, that sounds good. How much do I owe you, Jake?"

"Nothing. This stuff is left over from some of my other jobs. It wouldn't be right for me to charge you for scraps. Besides, I meant what I said when I told you that I want to help you get this farm up and running again."

Chase and Jake replaced one window frame at a time and Sally followed behind painting on the sealant. By the end of the day, they had all of the bad window frames replaced and a plan for replacing several exterior boards, which Chase would do during the week.

Glancing up at the darkening sky, she rubbed her shoulder. "Well, I forgot to eat lunch again today. This is quite possibly the best diet plan I've ever tried."

"You missed lunch again? Why didn't you say so? I would've brought some of Grandma's leftover fried chicken," Jake said.

"I have food. I was just too busy to eat. I need to head back home shortly. I have a two-hour drive tonight and work in the morning."

"If it's all right with you, I'd like to bring a buddy of mine over to check out your electrical wiring. I know you can't afford an electrician right now, but he's working on a job for me not far from here and won't charge much to take a quick look. You need to have it checked out before you have the power turned on."

"How much is not much?"

"Just let me worry about that. It's part of what general contractors handle. I'm your general contractor, right?" His smile was all charm.

She started to argue, but he cut her off. "Whether you've hired me or not, I'm your general contractor. This is what I do. Let me do this for you. You've always meant the world to me, and I'm going to help you. Besides, I owe your grandpa for teaching me to hunt, fish, and fix things when I was young. Dad was never around, and my own grandpa was too busy to mess with me. Your grandpa taught me a lot."

"But," Sally began.

"Please, Sally." The look of pain in his wide eyes melted her heart.

"Okay. I'm going to find a way to repay you when all of

this is finished." She resigned herself to the fact she needed all the help he was willing to provide.

"Good. We'll negotiate then." He tucked a lock of hair behind her ear. "I'm going to get the rest of the lumber, too. It'll be easier for me to haul it in my truck than for you to try to secure it to your car. Agreed?"

She nodded. "Be sure to keep your receipt because I plan to reimburse you when all of this is said and done."

"There is just one more thing. My buddy will need in the house during the week. Chase will, too. So, I need a key."

A bit dumbfounded, she stared at him for a moment before she spoke. "I only have one key."

"No problem. I can follow you into town on your way home, make a copy, and we're golden."

Reluctantly agreeing, she couldn't help but be impressed by the short amount of time it took the three of them to her load her car.

At the hardware store, she noticed a man giving Chase the stink eye and leaned over to the boy. "Who is that over by the anti-freeze display?"

"Uncle Ray. He hates me," Chase whispered back.

The man stomped over to where they stood and sneered. "What're you doing here, boy?"

"I'm doing some carpentry work for this lady. Uncle Ray, this is Miss Sally. She just bought the farm next to yours." The teen spoke with a hint of challenge.

Regarding him with cool composure, she extended her hand. "It's nice to meet you, Ray."

He mumbled something in return that she didn't quite catch and ignored her gesture of good will.

Jake inserted himself between them. "Chase will be home shortly. He's helping me with a few things. Christy knows he's with me."

Ray eyed Jake for a moment, grunted, and then stomped off.

The store clerk handed Sally the key. She slipped it into

Jake's hand. "I feel like I'm giving you the key to my life, Jake." Her tone betrayed her nervousness.

He looked deep into her eyes and responded, "I'll take very good care of it. Your life is precious to me." Then he kissed her forehead again.

She felt flushed all the way home. She couldn't stop thinking about Jake. It was late when she arrived and entered her dark, lonely house in the suburbs. She couldn't help but think how nice it would be if Jake was there with her. Dismissing that thought as fantasy, she prepared herself for the work week ahead.

CHAPTER 6

After a two-hour drive the following Friday evening, Sally arrived at the farmhouse with a car full of supplies. Most precious among her cargo were homemade peanut butter cookies for Chase and an apple pie for Jake. Amazed to find them working, illuminated by several battery powered work lights, she climbed out of her car.

"What are you guys doing here so late?"

"We wanted to surprise you, Miss Sally." Chase greeted her with a huge grin. "Come see what all I did this week."

The teen escorted her around the house with a bit of swagger. He showed her how most of the rotten boards and broken panes of glass were replaced. To her shock, her house had been completely rewired.

"Jake, why didn't you call me about the wiring?" she asked. "I assumed everything was fine since I didn't hear from you."

"My buddy checked it out and declared it unsafe. You had knob and tube wiring, which is dangerous enough.

What made it worse was a lot of it had been chewed by squirrels. Connecting the power would've been begging for a fire."

She felt the warmth leave her cheeks as her stomach heaved.

"Since he was working so close, he cut me a deal on installing Romex throughout." Jake's lips flattened as though he knew he was in for an argument.

Sally could see the dollar signs racking up and felt a little woozy. "How much did he charge?"

"Don't worry about it. I traded for most of it. He's doing some remodeling at his house and needed some things that I had in the shop. So, the bill was less than a good dinner in a nice restaurant." Jake gave her a big a smile, obviously pleased with himself.

She shook her head. "You cannot keep doing this. I feel like I'm taking advantage of you."

"Aren't you happy with the progress, Miss Sally?" Chase asked, his voice shaky. "Did we do something wrong?"

Her heart melted at the sad look on the boy's face. "No, sweetie. You didn't do anything wrong at all. You did a wonderful job. In fact, I have your cookies in the car. Let's go get them."

Chase's smile flashed as bright as the North Star when she handed him the large plastic container of cookies. "Thank you so much! May I have them now?"

"Sure. Those are yours to eat whenever you like." Seeing him so happy lightened her heart.

The young man ripped the lid off the container with gusto and moaned in pleasure when he took his first bite.

Laughing her earlier stress away, she said, "Well, I consider that a success. Oh, I made apple pie for you, Jake."

His face split with a huge smile, even white teeth gleaming in the harsh light. "You made me apple pie?

That's my favorite food in the entire world!"

"I remember. You couldn't get enough of it when we were kids." Her heart softened at the memory.

"It's the best food on the planet." He leaned in and took a big sniff of the dessert.

"You know," she began, "being here inspired me to bake pie. I could've sworn I smelled fresh baked apple pie in the house last weekend. I guess you could say I had a real hankering for it."

"You didn't tell me that." Jake leaned closer.

"Just my mind playing tricks on me because I was back in Grandma and Grandpa's house, I guess. A little down-home hallucination never hurt anyone, right?"

"No. It's weird because I smelled apple pie while I was helping my buddy rewire the house. I thought I was going nuts. Maybe that's your grandma's way of telling us she's glad to have us back. There are some things in this world that science will never explain."

"Personally, I think you belong here, Miss Sally. I can hardly wait until you're all moved in. You'll let me come visit, won't you?"

"Of course. You're always welcome here."

"Thank you. I feel real comfortable here with you and Jake. I don't feel that way with many people," Chase explained.

"Well, I think you're a great guy," Sally responded. "The house looks fabulous. I can't believe you got so much done in a week. Are you allowing enough time to study and work your paying job? I don't want to cut into your time."

"I only work a few hours a week at the store, and I do fine in school. I get my homework done in study hall. Aunt Christy says it's good for me to come here because it keeps me out of trouble."

"How is Christy, anyway?" Sally asked. "I haven't seen her since we were kids younger than you are now."

"She's okay. She works super hard and worries a lot.

She's never said so, but I know I'm a burden to her. She really doesn't have room for me in her little house. I tend to eat a lot because I have a big appetite. People say mean things to her about me. Most folks think she should toss me out on the street because I'm a bad seed from an evil apple."

"Bad seed? Who the hell called you that?" Sally was incensed at the idea of such cruelty toward a child.

Jake slipped his arm around her shoulders and whispered, "Down, Sweetness. It's just idle gossip from old church ladies with nothing better to do than tear down other folks."

Tears filled her eyes as she pulled away from Jake and wrapped her arms around the boy. "You're not a bad seed at all, Chase. In fact, I would be proud to call you my family. I'm sure your aunt feels the same way, whether or not she says so."

"Oh, Aunt Christy loves me. No doubt. It would just be better for her and the kids if I wasn't around."

"People will always talk," Jake interjected. "You have to learn to ignore them. Christy and your cousins love you. That's what matters. You just be the best person that you can, and don't worry about what anyone says."

Sally's respect for Jake raised a couple notches upon hearing his encouraging words. Chase was a sweet young man. No one should be bad-mouthing him or standing in judgment of him for events in which he had no part.

The boy glanced at his phone and grimaced. "I need to be getting home now. Aunt Christy wanted me home in time for her to go to her Bible study meeting. I watch the kids while she goes. It's the only time she goes out, so I can't fault her. Would it be okay for me to leave my cookies here so there's no way for my cousin to be exposed?"

"Of course. We'll put them in the kitchen for you. Do you need a ride?" Sally asked.

"No, ma'am. My horse is grazing in your north pasture. It's right on my way home. Aunt Christy's land borders yours," Chase said.

Sally hugged the kid and held him close for a moment. "You be safe going home. Do you need a flashlight or anything?"

"No, I see okay in the dark. Thank you, though. You're a nice lady. I hope only good things happen for you," Chase said and turned to walk toward the north pasture. Minutes later, Sally heard a horse whinny followed by hoof beats.

CHAPTER 7

"Thank you for introducing me to that kid, Jake," Sally said. "He needs some kindness."

"We all need kindness, Sweetness. Even you." He patted her shoulder. "So, I'd appreciate it if you didn't stress out about paying me for every little thing. Just let me be kind to you. Okay?"

"There's a difference between being kind and over doing things. You're over doing things, and I will repay you. Eventually," Sally said.

He fell silent for a few moments and then abruptly said, "Let's get your car unloaded, so we can go to dinner."

"Dinner?"

"Yes, I'd like to take out to dinner tonight. Unless you have other plans?"

"My only plans were to unpack my supplies, go over my list, and clean some more. You don't need to feed me. I'll be fine," she protested.

"You aren't understanding me. I want to take you to dinner just to take you to dinner. You know, some people call it a date." He leaned in close enough she could smell the Irish Spring soap on his skin.

"You want to take me out on a date?" She felt the blood rush to her face.

"I don't know why you seem so shocked. Is the idea of us together so mindboggling?"

"Well, no. I just never knew you felt that way," she whispered.

"The fact is you're the girl who got away, and I can't stand the thought of wasting any more time now that I've found you again."

"I'm the girl who . . .," Sally whispered. "Jake, are you telling me that you had feelings for me other than friendship when we were younger?"

Pink stole into Jake's sculpted cheeks as he replied, "Yeah. I did have feelings for you and they never quite went away. I've been carrying a torch for you since before we lost our baby teeth."

The revelation shocked her all the way to her shoes. "I had no idea. I'm sorry."

"Don't be sorry. Just say yes. Say yes to my dinner invitation. Say yes to my help with the farm. Say yes to me. Please, say yes. I realize that we don't even really know each other anymore, but I'd like the opportunity to get to know you again."

"You want to help too much," Sally said. "I don't want to take advantage of your kindness. It isn't fair to you."

"I want you to be able to move in and breathe life back into this place. I can save you a ton of time and frustration if you let me," Jake replied. "Please accept my help. Accept me."

She gasped for breath, her pulse racing as she became hyper aware of how closely they stood to each other.

"Oh, you big lug, I accept you. I've always accepted you," she whispered, her breath fanning his slightly parted lips.

He wasted no time in closing the distance between them. He slid one of his hands into her hair while the other lovingly cupped her face. His lips met hers in a sweet and gentle kiss. He moved his lips slowly and carefully as if she was something rare to savor. Sally moaned into his mouth, which he took as encouragement and slipped his tongue past her lips. He tasted her thoroughly as his hand left her face and trailed down her neck to her waist. He pressed her tightly against him. She could feel his heartbeat through his shirt, and his heat warmed her all the way to her toes.

Jake pulled away slightly, resting his forehead against hers. "I've been dreaming about doing that for many years now."

She smiled, still trying to catch her breath. "Well, if I'd had any idea you were dreaming about kissing me, I would have hunted you down a long time ago so you could make it a reality."

He stared into her eyes for a few moments before speaking. "Just so we're clear, you and I are dating now. Right?"

She giggled like a teenaged girl. "It sounds like dating to me. Geez, I feel like I'm in high school again."

Jake pulled her to him and claimed her lips fiercely. His arms completely encompassed her as he pressed her firmly into the warmth of his body. His tongue demanded entrance into the deepest recesses of her mouth where he tasted every last inch of her.

He pulled away leaving her gasping for breath. "Now, what do you say to dinner?"

"I'd love to have dinner with you." She looked down at her plain sweater. "I don't look very good, though. I didn't bring anything nice with me. I was expecting to work on the house all weekend."

"You look great to me." Jake said gently. "You taste great, too."

She took a deep breath and then stopped breathing.

"Jake, do you smell apple pie?"

Jake sniffed the air and grinned. "Yeah. Your grandma approves of us together."

"Well, Grandma always did like you." She looped her arm through his. "I'm suddenly very hungry."

CHAPTER 8

They walked into the Italian restaurant hand in hand. The place had a casual atmosphere, so Sally didn't feel too awkward in her jeans and sweater. The lighting was dim, and the tables were spaced far enough apart to offer intimacy.

They were shown to a table with a view of the lake. It was the perfect place to enjoy quiet conversation while the ripples in the water sparkled like fairy lights.

"I didn't know Elderberry had any cozy restaurants like this. It's been a long time, but I guess I didn't expect anything to change around here." She shook her head. "I know it's stupid, but in my mind, everything is still as it was when we were kids."

"Well, places change and grow. So do people. I've changed and grown a lot." Jake grinned, his intelligent eyes studying her. "I'm not the shy kid you knew. I sit before you now a grown man who isn't afraid to go after what he wants. That's why my business is successful. I won't allow it to fail." He leaned back in his chair. Candlelight cast shadows on his strong jaw, and his eyes held a level of warmth she'd never seen before.

"What would you like this evening?" the young female server asked Jake.

"Her," he answered without taking his gaze off Sally.

"Sir, I don't think she's on the menu," the server replied with a small knowing smile.

Sally burst out laughing. "He'll have the chicken fettuccini, and I'll have the lasagna."

The girl's brows rose as she looked at Sally. She turned to Jake. "Is that okay? You want the chicken fettuccini?"

He glanced up at the girl and smiled. "This lady knows just what I like. Chicken fettuccini is exactly what I want. And a bottle of your best champagne. Thank you."

She slipped away, leaving them alone. He made her feel like the most beautiful woman in the world. He stared deeply into her eyes with an intensity that made her think of hot nights and silk sheets.

She cleared her throat and was about to speak when she heard a nasally voice behind her say, "So, little Sally Sue is back. Isn't that just great? Are you enjoying my farm?"

She turned to find her cousin, Danny, hovering over her. His upper lip curled into a sneer and his close-set brown eyes were narrowed in hate. Too shocked to respond right away, she stared at the last person she'd expected to see this evening.

"The farm is Sally's," Jake said in a commanding voice. "You lost it. She bought it. End of story. Now scram."

"I was robbed! The county didn't give me a chance to pay those taxes." Danny's voice rose higher and higher with each word. "They wouldn't work with me. By all rights, that place is mine!"

Sally drew a deep calming breath and stood to face her distant cousin. "Danny, I'm truly sorry that you lost the property, but it's clear you never once set foot on the place after you inherited it. You just let it decay. I bought it fair and square. I paid cash for it. The premises is now mine and will remain mine because I know how to take care of my business. I'm sorry, but your failure was my opportunity."

"You snooty cow!" His face reddened, and his cheeks puffed out as he hissed, "You always have thought you were better than everyone else."

She took another deep breath. "No. I don't think I'm better than anyone. I just happen to be more responsible than you. If you will excuse us, Jake and I would like to get back to our evening." She sat back down and eyed him over the top of her glass as she took a sip of champagne.

Danny opened his mouth to reply, but clamped his lips closed when Jake rose to his full height. He towered over the bitter, quivering man. "Have a good night." Jake's voice carried a lethal tone.

Danny turned to her and whispered, "This isn't the end, Sally Sue. Not by a long shot. You'll regret taking my property. You'll pay dearly for stealing from me!"

Jake glowered at Danny and said, "If you mess with Sally, you are messing with me. Just remember that before you do anything stupid. I've let you get by with a lot before she came back. I won't be so magnanimous if you mess with Sally."

Danny's face reddened, and he scurried off, leaving Sally staring at Jake in bewilderment.

"It's sounds like you and Danny have an unresolved issue."

"It's not important right now. What's important is that I don't trust the little snake to keep his distance. I don't want you staying at the farm alone until we get the place more secured. Someone should really be there every day. I can probably talk Chase into staying there during the week, and I can stay on the weekends." Jake rubbed his temple as he reclaimed his seat.

"Are you saying that you think Danny would try to hurt

me?"

"Yeah. I know he would if he thought he could get away with it. You aren't going to argue with me on this, are you?"

Sally thought for a moment before responding. "No, I'm not going to argue with you about this. I'd appreciate the company until I can at least get a watch dog."

"Good. I'll call Chase and see if he's on board. I have a feeling he will be all over this. Those two have some bad blood."

He stepped away to make his phone call but stayed within sight of the table.

"Chase agreed to stay at your house but wants to move in immediately. It seems he and Ray have been arguing since he got home. It doesn't hurt that he's taken quite a liking to you," Jake said.

"I don't have any power yet. He wouldn't be very comfortable until there's electricity."

"Chase told me that he doesn't want Danny anywhere near a nice lady like you. He's more than ready to stay there. All he asks is that you keep making cookies for him."

She opened her mouth to reply, but the food arrived, distracting her with the amazing aroma. She accepted her plate and ate with zeal, momentarily forgetting that she was on a date.

She glanced up to find Jake grinning at her. She slowly put her fork down and dabbed her lips with her napkin. "I'm sorry. I got a bit carried away. I really love lasagna." She studied her plate, aghast at how much she'd already eaten.

"I love a woman with healthy appetites, so please, eat up. Don't ever pretend to be someone you aren't." The quirk of his lips made her think of the big bad wolf from a fairytale.

"What time is Chase supposed to be over?" she asked.

"His aunt is at Bible study until about ten o'clock. So, it

will be after that," Jake murmured.

"We should hurry if we want to be there before he arrives." Sally renewed her efforts to shovel her food down her throat.

Jake gave her a long look before wolfing down his fettuccini. He was finished in less than five minutes and requesting the check. He paid their bill and made good time getting back to the farm.

CHAPTER 9

"I brought an air mattress with me. It's in my trunk," Sally said fidgeting as Jake parked the truck in her driveway.

"We can get it later, but I have a different idea right now." He reached behind the seat of the truck and withdrew a large red and black plaid blanket. "Come with me. There's someplace I want to show you."

Jake led her down a deer path to a tranquil, secluded spot alongside a broad stream. The moon sat low in the sky like a huge gold coin, its reflection shimmering on the water. Brilliant stars twinkled overhead.

"I've wanted to bring you here since I began to notice the difference between boys and girls. You're the only woman I've ever wanted to share this with." He spread the blanket on the soft grass beside the creek.

"It's beautiful. I didn't know my grandparents had such a place." Sally glanced around with wide eyes.

"It's actually on my grandma's land. I stumbled across this spot one day when I was looking for one of her dogs that ran off. The moment I saw it, I knew I wanted to share it with someone special."

He leaned closer to claim her lips with a kiss. It seemed to her that she'd always known the taste and feel of his lips. Too soon, he broke the contact, leaving her with a terrible hunger to taste him again.

This powerful man shows me such gentleness. I could lose myself in him if I'm not careful.

He leaned over and kissed her on the forehead before shaking out the folded blanket and spreading it out on the ground. He lowered his long body onto the soft material and held his hand out to her.

"Would you like to join me for a few minutes of star gazing?"

"Isn't it a bit chilly for star gazing?" She fought to keep her breathing even.

"Trust me. I will keep you warm, Sweetness," he whispered in a husky voice.

She knelt on the blanket beside him and lowered herself to lie next to him. He chased away all traces of the autumn chill the moment he slipped his arm around her and pulled her against his side. For a moment, she went perfectly still. Silence stretched between them, broken only by the sound of water gushing down the creek.

Could this man be my soulmate, my love?

"There's the Big Dipper." He pointed to the constellation.

She examined the sky and then pointed. "Is that Saturn?"

"I think so. Let's see what else we can find." He turned and kissed her temple.

They were cuddled together in the quiet when Sally popped up to stare at the sky. "Oh, Jake, look at the shooting stars! Is it a meteor shower? I've never seen one with such clarity."

"A lot more stars are visible out here than you can see in

the city. Street lights mute the brilliance of the night sky. Make a wish bathed in starlight, and it might come true."

She inhaled swiftly and let it out slowly. "Jake, that's a beautiful thing to say. It's poetic. I haven't been anywhere this peaceful in years."

Jake opened his mouth to say something, but was interrupted by a wolf howl in the distance. He tilted his head to listen for a minute and then reluctantly got up. He reached down and pulled her to her feet.

"I'm sorry, Sally, but we need to get back to the house."

"What's wrong?" Confused by his sudden change in demeanor, she asked, "Did I do something wrong?"

He turned to her and traced his fingers down her cheek, tucking a lock of hair behind her ear. "No, Sweetness. How could you even think that? We just need to get back to the house. I'm sure Chase is there by now."

"Okay, then." Still feeling bewildered, she folded the blanket and followed him back up the trail.

When the path widened, he slipped his arm around her shoulders and snuggled her firmly to his side.

She was shocked to see a glow coming from the windows as they neared the house. They climbed up on the porch steps just as Chase swung the door open. He looked Sally over from head to toe with eyes that gleamed with merriment.

"Hi, you two. Did you have a nice walk this evening?"

"Yes, we did," Jake snarled, "and we don't want to talk about it."

Chase smiled bigger. "I brought some oil lanterns that I've set up in every room along with some other supplies. I already lit the fire and set up my stuff in the back bedroom."

"There's no heat back there," she protested. "I'm afraid you'll get too cold."

"I'll be fine, Miss Sally. Thank you for worrying about me, though. I'm not used to folks doing that." The youth ducked his head, his cheeks pink.

"Chase," Jake's baritone voice boomed, "thank you for coming to stay here. I feel much better knowing a young man such as yourself will be watching over things."

"Miss Sally is special," Chase said, protectiveness written in the set of his jaw and gleam in his eyes. "She should be protected from the likes of Danny the shyster. I'm only too happy to help."

Jake turned to Sally. "You do understand that I'm also staying with you tonight. Right?"

"I thought we already discussed that." She couldn't stifle the sigh that escaped her lips.

So much for nonchalance.

"Where's that air mattress you mentioned earlier?"

"It's in my trunk. I'll go get it." Sally headed for the door.

She saw Chase shake his head at Jake just before he said, "I'll be happy to get it for you, Miss Sally. You and Jake probably want a minute to yourselves, anyway. Where are your keys?"

She reached into her pocket and withdrew her keyring. She handed them over reluctantly. With a nod to Jake, the teen went outside to retrieve her air mattress.

"So, is there room for two on that inflatable bed of yours, or do you want me to sleep on the floor?" Jake's lips curved into a devilish smile.

"There's room on the air mattress if the two people are cozy together." She felt her cheeks grow warm and knew she was blushing. "I would never ask you to sleep on the floor. It's still filthy. I've swept, but I haven't mopped yet."

"Oh, I think we can be real cozy together," Jake said as his mouth took her lips in a warm sweet kiss. He pulled away after a long moment, his lips hovering a mere inch above hers. "In fact, I think we could probably share your sleeping bag if we had to."

"Um, do you want this in the first bedroom or in front of

the fire, Miss Sally?" Chase asked red-faced, refusing to look either of them in the eye.

Still holding her close, Jake answered for her. "In front of the fire would be great. We don't want our Sally getting cold."

"No, sir," the teen rasped. "I'm sure she'll be plenty warm tonight."

Chase set the mattress down on the floor near the natural stone hearth and then turned to Jake. "Can I have a word with you real quick before I turn in?"

"Yeah, I'd like a word with you, too," Jake mumbled.

The two men eyed each other as they walked through the door and out of earshot.

Sally busied herself with the bicycle pump she'd brought to inflate the air mattress while they had their little man talk.

She was pumping as fast as her arms would allow when the guys came back inside. "What the hell are you doing?" Jake asked thrusting his arms out wide.

"I'm inflating the mattress. What does it look like I'm doing?" she snapped.

"I have an air compressor in my truck. Let me have that thing. I'll have it ready for you in a jiffy." The brooding man stalked out the door, dragging her limp mattress along.

After the door clicked shut, she turned back to find her young guest staring at her. His gaze was soft with concern.

"What's on your mind?"

"Well, I've known Jake my whole life. He's a good man, but I don't know how he is with women. I've never seen him with a woman." The kid blushed, put his hands in his pockets, and ducked his head. "He never came around here when he was married to Mary."

"I'm sure he treats women just fine." She laid her hand on his shoulder.

"Well, you're a special lady. If he isn't good to you, I want to know. Not that I'm trying to take you from him or anything. I don't want that, but sometimes a woman just needs a friend to look out for her. You know?"

"Thank you for looking out for me, sweetie. I'm sure Jake will treat me well. He certainly has so far. But if something changes, I'm a big girl. You aren't responsible for me." Sally looked the young man in the eye. "I can't imagine him ever hurting me on purpose."

"I never would," Jake boomed from the door, dragging in the inflated air mattress. "Chase, you've no cause to worry. There is no scenario that would ever cause me to hit Sally the way your dad hit your mom. It won't happen. You can relax. Her wellbeing is very important to me."

Chase hung his head and looked ashamed. "I'm sorry," he mumbled. "I just worry."

"Don't be sorry," Sally said with a smile. "I appreciate your concern, and I want you to know that I'm touched you care enough to offer me your protection. I don't take that kind of thing lightly."

"She's right," Jake said. "You should never be ashamed of looking out for someone. I'm happy that you have her back."

"Jake, you're a good man." The teen nodded to older guy. "I hope you two will be very happy together."

"Chase," Sally began, "what makes you think that we're together?"

"I can scent, I mean, sense it. I just sense that you guys became a couple tonight. Am I wrong?"

Sally felt Jake's scrutiny as she answered, "No, you're not wrong. I was just curious as to how you knew."

"Oh, I just have a nose for that type of thing. I'm going to head to bed now. I'll see you two in the morning. Good night." The kid scampered off as quick as his legs could take him.

"Good night," Sally called to him.

She felt her cheeks heat with the knowledge that she was about to share a bed with Jake for the first time. She looked up at him and found him gazing back at her with a soft smile and loving eyes. She felt her heart melt right there.

CHAPTER 10

"Do you have sheets or something that you want on that thing?" Jake asked.

"Yes, they're in a bag in my backseat." Her voice was barely above a whisper. "I'll get them."

She let a squeak of surprise as Jake's hand reached out and caught her wrist in the blink of an eye. "I'm sorry. I didn't mean to startle you. I'll get everything from your car. You just sit tight right here."

He kissed her forehead and dashed out the door. He soon returned with all of her bags in tow.

Placing the bags on the floor, he opened the one with the sheets, obvious due the pillow case peeking out the top. He made quick work of putting them on the inflated bed while Sally carried her bag of clothes into the bedroom and set it on the floor.

Back in the other room, she busied herself unpacking the large bag, which was full of cleaning supplies, non-perishable food, and materials for the house. She put everything in the kitchen cabinets and on the kitchen table she'd just cleaned. Looking around, she realized how much work Chase had done on the place over the past week.

She slipped into the bedroom and changed into a pair of baggy sweat pants, a comfy T-shirt, and warm socks. She blew out the oil lamp, thankful Chase had been so proactive. Upon returning to the living room, the sight of Jake sprawled out on the bed wearing nothing but his black silk boxers and a sleepy smile greeted her hungry gaze.

"Is that how you plan to sleep?" she whispered.

"Yeah. I hope it won't be a problem. I know we're still getting to know each other again, so I have no plans of ravishing you tonight." Jake gave her a rakish grin. "Of course, I might reconsider if you ask me nicely."

With a blush burning to the roots of her hair, she said, "Yes, it's a problem. I can't sleep next to you like that. Your offer is tantalizing, but I think we should wait on that for a little while."

She snagged one of the lit lanterns and scurried to the bedroom, her cheeks burning and mind racing with the image of him sprawled out on her bed wearing nothing but boxers. She rummaged through her open suitcase and grasped the biggest thing she could find, a thick pair of pink sweatpants. She returned to the living room and tossed them to him.

"I'm really tired. I'd appreciate it if you'd put those on, so I can sleep in peace."

"Pink?" He held the fabric between his thumb and index finger like it might bite him.

She couldn't suppress her grin at his raised brows and severe frown.

"It's the only thing I have big enough to fit you. I'm sorry if the color offends you." She couldn't help herself, she giggled.

His shoulders slumped with his sigh, but he pulled the fleece over his long legs and up to his waist. The ankle bands hugged his shins as he straightened. He stared at them for a moment before he burst out laughing, which made Sally laugh.

"You should be comfy and warm all night in those." She gasped as the struggled for breath.

"I was never worried about that." He plopped down on the bed and opened his arms. "Come here, and let me hold you tonight."

Sally blew out the lamp and snuggled into his arms, which he wrapped around her with a gentleness she didn't know was possible. Resting her head on his chest, she sighed in contentment with the warmth and safety his big body offered. Although he didn't speak again, she sensed conflict inside him and pulled him closer.

His whisker stubble was rough against her temple as his breathing evened out and sleep claimed him.

I was right. He does keep a woman toasty warm and comfortable. I could sure get used to this.

She let sleep take her and dreamed of two wolves. The black one was young and rambunctious. The white one was bigger and looked older. They loped around her house like watch dogs, taking turns patrolling the area. Coming closer, they sniffed at the porch steps. A few seconds later, the bigger wolf climbed the steps to the door and started contorting.

He twisted, his bones popping and changing until he became a human male. The man was naked and let himself into her house where he stood and gazed at her sleeping form. Then he slid into bed with her. When she turned to push him away, she found herself staring into Jake's face, his blue eyes searching for an answer to an unasked question.

Sally startled awake, sitting straight up in bed with a little cry. Beside her, Jake became instantly alert, scanning the room for threats. "What's wrong?"

Chase barreled through the door from the back bedroom wearing a t-shirt and gym shorts. Wild-eyed, he looked like he was ready to take on a grizzly bear with nothing but a fork.

"What happened?"

"I'm sorry to wake you guys. I just had a weird dream. It's not anything to worry about," she mumbled, hiding her face against Jake's chest.

"Tell us about it." Jake spoke softly, rubbing soothing circles on her back.

"I really don't want to. It's nothing. I have a fanciful imagination, which gives me odd dreams sometimes. Let's go back to sleep. I'm sorry to worry you guys."

Chase sat down on the side of the mattress, regarding her with a seriousness that belied his young years. "Sometimes dreams are our mind's way of telling us things we need to know."

"How did you get so wise at your age?" She sighed.

"Mom always said it was my Native American blood. Said I inherited something special from my ancestors. Nobody else has ever called me wise." He shifted, looking uncomfortable with the praise.

Jake slid his arms around her and brought her closer to his warm body. "Tell us about your dream. It'll make you feel better."

"If you insist. I'll give you the short version. There were two wolves circling my house. They were sniffing around and seemed to be making sure everything was okay. One of the wolves climbed onto the porch and transformed into a man. Then the man came into the house and got in bed with me. When I looked at him, he was you, Jake," Sally said with a small laugh. "Just a weird dream, right?"

Jake and Chase shared a long look before Chase said, "I'm going to head back to bed now. I'm glad you're okay, Miss Sally."

"I'm sorry I woke you. Just ignore me."

"Miss Sally, I'm here to protect you and your place. You were threatened tonight by an evil little man who is above nothing. When you cry out like that, I'm going to come investigate. That's why I'm here." He turned and walked back toward his room with a straight back and determined pace.

Looking at Jake, she said, "He's taking this protection business very seriously, isn't he? He's better than an alarm system."

Jake stared deeply into her eyes before replying. "He's supposed to take your safety seriously. That's why I called him. He has an unpleasant history with Danny. I'll let him tell you about that when he's ready, but suffice to say that he knows what your slimy cousin is capable of. He'd take great pleasure in stopping anything Danny tried to do to you."

Her head fell against his shoulder in exhaustion. He kissed the top of her head. "We'll talk more in the morning. Right now, let's get some more sleep. You and I have a lot to discuss very soon."

He was snoring softly again within a few minutes. Listening to the comforting rumble of his sleep, she closed her eyes and reached for sleep. Her racing mind kept her from the solace of slumber. Her confused feelings haunted and taunted her as she fought to sort them.

Something drew her and Jake together. They hadn't seen each other in several years, but it felt as though they'd never been apart. She wanted him, but it was more than physical desire. She wanted his mind, body, and heart. They already had a deep connection. Could they have a future together? Was this destiny? Is that why she felt such an instant and powerful attraction to him?

She adjusted her pillow and once again tried to quiet her thoughts. Images of Danny's crazed eyes brought a tingle of fear to her spine. Would he really harm her, or worse, Jake? Life is short. What if she and Jake never had an opportunity to explore what was between them? What could that tingle of electricity she felt from him mean?

What if the secret she sensed inside him was enough to keep them apart?

She was sure he'd share his secret with her someday. No matter what mystery he protected, nothing could surprise her more than his seduction of her heart. She'd never planned to get involved with anyone after the bitterness of her divorce. She'd promised herself that she wouldn't allow her heart to be captured again. Yet here was Jake, lying next to her with his arm draped over her waist, his breath fanning her face.

Could she take a chance and love him? Let him love her? She imagined a life with him. He would keep her on her toes, never letting her dwell too long on anything. He was a man of action, and his instinct was to fix what was broken. Even if the broken thing was her spirit.

She snuggled further into his warmth and felt his arm tighten around her. "Sally. My Sweetness," he mumbled in his sleep. Her name was drawn out on his lips as if he were tasting the syllables. It sounded poetic, almost like a prayer.

CHAPTER 11

S ally awoke to the smell of bacon wafting through the house.

That's strange. I didn't bring any bacon.

She got up and wandered into the kitchen where she found Chase grilling bacon on a portable grill just outside the back door. She opened the door and breathed deeply. The aroma filled her with a sense of home and rightness.

"Good morning, Chase," she said, her voice rough from sleep. "Where did the bacon come from?"

He flashed a big grin at her. "A pig, Miss Sally. Bacon comes from pigs."

She laughed good and loud. "I know where bacon comes from. I was just wondering how this particular bacon got here to your grill."

"Oh, Jake brought it from Mrs. Hill's house. He brought eggs, too. I thought we would cook those in the bacon grease," he said with another bright smile.

"That sounds glorious! The only thing we're missing is coffee."

"I've got coffee in the thermos," Jake said from behind her. "Grandma fixed it for us when I ran up to take care of her cattle this morning. She even sent three coffee mugs. She doesn't believe in drinking from disposable cups. Says it ruins the flavor."

"Well, who am I to argue with Mrs. Hill? This is amazing. I was planning to have a granola bar and a bottle of water for breakfast."

Chase placed the bacon on a plate with a pink rose border that screamed Mrs. Hill before cracking eggs into the bacon grease. Jake poured hot, aromatic coffee into a mug adorned with pretty pink roses that said "Mom" on the front.

He handed the mug to Sally, and said, "This is yours because Chase and I just aren't Mom material."

Sally's face fell and she withdrew from the guys. "I wanted to be a mom, but it wasn't in the cards for me."

"You can be my mom, Miss Sally," Chase said from behind her. "I don't have one anymore."

Tears pricked the backs of her eyes, and she ran to hug him tightly. "I'm sorry. I heard your mom left a few years ago."

"Yeah, but I don't think she left of her own free will. I think someone took her. I just don't believe that she would leave me like that. She was a very good mom. Always shielding me from Dad when he got drunk. My dad was one mean drunk."

"You think she was kidnapped?" Sally asked.

"Maybe kidnapped. Maybe worse. I know one thing, though. My mom didn't run away from my dad and abandon me. If she was going to run, she would have taken me with her."

"How old were you when this happened?" Sally asked.

"I was ten years old. There's no way my mom would have left me."

"How old are you now?" Sally studied the teen who had

eyes that had seen so much sorrow.

"I just turned sixteen. I still have two years of school left. I promised Aunt Christy that I'd leave as soon as I finished high school, if not before. She says I can stay as long as I like, but I know it's not fair to her."

"Your aunt doesn't want you at her house?"

"It's not that she doesn't love me or anything. It's just that she has her own kids to worry about, and I take up space and eat a lot. She loves that I've been working here the past week. She was really happy to hear that I'll be staying here for a while. It gives her a little breathing room, I think."

Shoulders slumped, he turned to tend the eggs just outside the kitchen door. Jake rested his hands on her shoulders while she stared after the young man.

"It's not unheard of to adopt a sixteen-year-old boy, is it?" She chewed her bottom lip, her mind racing.

"He's legally not an adult yet, so I'm sure it can be done," he said. "Would you seriously consider adopting him? He's a good boy, but that's still a hell of a responsibility."

"Once I'm settled a bit, I may look into it. I wonder if Christy is his legal guardian since his dad's in jail or if he's a ward of the state. There's a lot to consider," Sally said.

"Well, you're a sweet woman for even contemplating adopting him," Jake said and then kissed her temple.

Chase came back into the house carrying a plate loaded with fried eggs. They all sat down at the ancient Formica table and enjoyed a hearty breakfast.

"So, Miss Sally, what would you like for me to do today?"

"Well, we need to replace the rest of the rotten boards and then finish cleaning up in here. We need to decide what's staying and what's going. The sunken couch needs to go. I don't think there's any saving it. The rocking chair might be salvageable. I think I can have a seat put back on it. The kitchen table and chairs are staying for sure. They hold so many wonderful childhood memories for me. I won't know if any of the appliances still work until I get power, which I'll try to get turned on this week."

"Okay, we can probably get the boards replaced today. Then I'll start cleaning, and this place will be spotless by the time you come back next weekend. Once the power comes on, I can check your appliances if you like," Chase said.

"That would be great. Thank you for everything you've done and are going to do. You're moving this project along way ahead of schedule."

"Miss Sally, I'm having a really great time doing things around here. It's so nice to be trusted to get something done and not have someone looking over my shoulder, criticizing everything I do."

"Chase, I realize that I haven't known you for very long, but I haven't seen you do a single thing for which you should be criticized. You're polite, helpful, enthusiastic, charming, smart, and will be an ace carpenter someday if that's what you really want to do. You're one of those guys who could do just about anything you want in life. I'm beyond happy that you've decided to help me get the farm going. Now pay close attention to me when I tell you that you are welcome here any time. Not just during this renovation phase. Ten years from now, you'll still be just as welcome here as you are today. Remember that. I don't issue those open invitations lightly."

"Thank you, Miss Sally," Chase whispered just before he surprised her with a fierce hug. "I haven't been welcome anywhere in a really long time."

"Any time, Chase. I mean it." Her firm tone brooked no argument. "Now, enough mushy stuff. Let's get started."

They cleared the table and stacked the dirty dishes in Mrs. Hill's picnic basket since they had no way to wash them. Since there wasn't any leftover food to pack, there was no hurry to return the basket.

These men have really hearty appetites. I'm going to spend a fortune on food. Having them around will be worth it, though.

CHAPTER 12

The day flew by, each of them tending to a different project. By dusk, all of the rotten boards were replaced, the windows had been repaired and cleaned, and the appliances checked for rodent nests and insects.

"I'll set off a bug bomb before I go to school on Monday," Chase told Sally that evening as they were sitting in front of the fire enjoying peanut butter sandwiches and apple cider warmed on the hearth.

"That sounds like a great plan," Jake said.

Chase started to respond but went silent, his mouth still agape. Jake stilled, as well. They both turned toward the door like they were listening to something.

"Is the back door locked?" Jake whispered.

"I don't think so," Sally answered. "Why are we whispering?"

"Because you have an uninvited visitor, Miss Sally," Chase said. "Do you think he'll come to the door like a man or try something underhanded?" he asked Jake.

"My truck is parked behind the house where we unloaded supplies earlier. I bet he thinks Sally's here alone. He's going to try something sneaky. I'm willing to bet on it."

Just then they heard heavy footfalls climbing the porch steps.

"Well, it appears I was wrong," Jake whispered. "Chase, I would rather he not know that we're here. I want to see what he has up his sleeve. So, you and I are going to step into the front bedroom where we have a good view of Sally and can hear every word."

She started to say something, but was interrupted by an aggressive knock at the door. "Sally Sue, you thief, I know you're in there. Open the door!"

Sally straightened her spine and marched to the door. Opening it just enough to peer out she asked, "What brings you here? Did you come to help me clean up this place?"

"Whatever," Danny sniveled as he pushed his way past her and into the living room. "I came to warn you to leave. This place is mine. You have no business here."

"Listen very carefully. This property was purchased by my grandparents. They sank their life savings into this land. They nurtured the farm and turned it into a thriving enterprise. For whatever reason, they left it to your dad. He did nothing with it. He simply sold or took everything of value."

She took a deep breath. "Then you inherited it. You haven't done anything to keep it up. Have you even seen the barn? The whole thing needs to come down." Sally planted her feet and propped her hands on her hips. "You and your father neglected this farm. Then you lost it. News flash, Danny, grownups have to pay taxes or they lose their property. You didn't pay your taxes, and now the farm is back in loving hands again."

"It's too bad you feel that way because you're going to die here." Danny's face twisted with an evil smile, his eyes taking on a crazed gleam. "If I can't have this place, then no one can! You won't live to see your next birthday if you stay here."

"Danny, don't you dare threaten me! You disgusting worm! You are on MY property! This place is MINE!" Sally dashed over to the old sunken couch. She reached behind it and grasped her rifle. In a flash, she had the safety off, ready to shoot. She took aim squarely at Danny's chest.

"What the hell are you doing with that thing?" Her cousin stumbled back a step. Beads of sweat sprouted on his upper lip and forehead. "You're going to hurt yourself. Little girls shouldn't play with guns."

"Don't kid yourself into thinking that I don't know how to use this. You came into my house and threatened to kill me. I will be calling the law to report it. You better leave now before I lose my temper."

He backed toward the door as she paced him. Sweat dripped down his face. "This isn't over. There's a reason your family was written out of the will. You were never meant to be here."

"Well, I'm here, anyway. If you wanted to keep the place, you should have thought of that before you failed to pay the taxes. What did you think would happen? You knew someone was going to buy this property. Why does it matter so much that it was me? Did you believe someone would buy it and never bother to do anything with it?" Sally's voice rose to a powerful pitch.

"You don't belong here! You're the one who needs to leave!" Danny's voice reached a high-pitched squeal.

Taking a step closer, she snarled, "Get out of my house, and don't you ever come back!" The sudden flash of fear in his eyes encouraged her.

With one last sneer, he turned and slunk out the door. Following him to the front porch, she kept her gun trained on him until the taillights from his car disappeared from sight. Satisfied he was gone, she lowered her weapon and walked back inside.

Jake and Chase were standing just inside the door. Jake's face was red with fury, and Chase had a restraining hand on his arm. "Miss Sally, are you okay?" the young man asked.

"I think so. I'm so angry, though. I could have killed him. I really wanted to shoot him." She shook her head. "That isn't like me. Danny really pushes my buttons."

"I already called the sheriff," Jake said pulling away from Chase and slipping his arm around her shoulders. "He's on his way to take your statement." He hugged her closer to his body. "I wanted to tear that little weasel apart. Chase had the presence of mind to stop me, so we could try to figure out his scheme. Then you grabbed the gun and took control. You've turned into quite a little warrior."

"I'll always defend myself. I'm no shrinking violet. He threatened me. My own cousin threatened me over property that he never even used. I don't understand." She slipped her arms around Jake's waist and held on tight.

"I've never understood anything he did," Chase said scratching his head. "He used to come around Mom quite a bit when Dad wasn't home. She'd send him packing, but he always came back. He never learned."

Sally took a deep breath to try to calm down. Then she stopped short. "Do you guys smell lanolin? The kind that Grandpa used to use?"

Jake and Chase both inhaled and looked at each other puzzled. "Yeah, that's lanolin," Chase answered.

"Where in the world is that smell coming from?" Jake asked.

"I don't know," Sally walked around the living room and looked in all of the corners as if a jar of lanolin would suddenly appear. "It's almost like Grandpa is here and letting us know he's with us."

Chase nodded. "Spirits often guard their loved ones. Just think of it as he's watching over you."

"Zeke should be here soon. Do you need some water or something?" Jake peered into her pale face.

Determined steps sounded on the porch followed by a short, firm knock.

Jake opened the door to a middle-aged man with silver hair, tan skin, and an otherworldly quality. He wore his sheriff's department uniform like it was an extension of himself.

"Zeke, it's good to see you," Jake said shaking his hand.

"Jake. Chase. Ma'am," the sheriff greeted them all, shaking hands with each in turn.

"Zeke, this is Sally Wagner. She's returned at long last to reclaim her rightful place as a farmer. Sally, this is Sheriff Zeke Meyers," Jake said making the introductions.

"I'm sorry to meet you under such circumstances, but I'm really happy you're here, Sheriff," Sally said.

"It's a pleasure to meet you, Ms. Wagner." The sheriff spoke in a smooth voice like aged whiskey. "Now tell me exactly what happened here."

She started off by telling him how Danny had threatened her in the restaurant and then shown up at the house and threatened her again. "He said if he couldn't have the farm that no one could, and I would die here."

"What did you do after he threatened you, Ms. Wagner?"

"I grabbed my gun and pointed it at his chest. He still argued with me and didn't want to leave. I got closer to him and yelled at him. He finally left, but he promised me that it wasn't over. Sheriff, I really think he wants me dead."

"I see. You might want to consider staying in a hotel while you work on the house. I certainly advise against you staying here by yourself," Sheriff Zeke said tapping his pen on his small notebook.

"I'm not alone. Jake and Chase are both staying here with me," Sally explained.

"Ah. In that case, I'm going to need to contact Christy

about all of this since Chase is still a minor."

"Sheriff, please don't make this sound worse than it is. Aunt Christy is really happy that I'm here, so she can deal with Uncle Ray and the kids without me in the way." Chase's gaze was steady as he stared the Sheriff straight in the eye.

"All right, Chase. I won't try to convince her that you should go home. I know things are strained between you and Ray."

The sheriff looked around for a minute and then said, "Ms. Wagner, I admire what you're doing here. It'd be a real shame if Danny caused you to give up. I'll file your report and get a warrant for his arrest. You do need to be careful, though. Keep your doors and windows locked and that rifle handy. He grew up in these hills, and there are lots of places for him to hide."

"Please call me Sally. Yes, I'll be careful. Thank you for everything, Sheriff."

"Call me Zeke," he said with a kind smile.

"I'll walk you out, Zeke," Jake offered. The two men disappeared out the door while having a quiet discussion.

Sally turned to Chase. "Maybe you should go home. I don't want anything happening to you because you're here with me."

"No, Miss Sally. You need me here. Now more than ever. Very few people know Danny like me. He's a viper who waits for you to turn your back and then strikes."

"What did he do to you, Chase?" Sally sat on the side of the air mattress and patted the spot next to her. After a moment he joined her.

"He tried to stop Aunt Christy from taking me in. He spread all sorts of lies about me. Said I was Dad's accomplice in the robbery. I was only ten years old. How could I have had anything to do with that?" He paused to collect his thoughts. "He convinced Uncle Ray I was a bad seed, would steal them blind, and would be the death of their marriage. He told people that I was a pathological liar with mental problems. Danny even talked to the Social Services case worker and told her I needed to be institutionalized." He put his elbows on his knees, resting his face in his hands. "I just don't know why he hates me so much."

She laid a comforting hand on his shoulder. "Do you have any idea why he did those things?"

"The only thing I can think of is he didn't want me talking about how he chased after my mom. Nobody believed me when I tried to tell them, anyway."

"I believe you. You have no reason to make something like that up." She rubbed small circles on his back.

Determination filled his eyes as he looked at her. "The man is evil, and I'm not going to let him hurt you. You've always been nice to me and treated me like a regular person. I don't know why Danny doesn't want you here, but I'm not letting him chase you off."

She couldn't help herself and wrapped her arms around him, holding him for a little while.

Jake returned and sat on the other side of Sally. He put his arms around the both of them. "That little weasel won't win this one. Zeke is calling in the pack. Er, I mean he's calling in reinforcements."

Chase nodded and shared a long look with Jake.

Sally shook her head wondering about Jake's slip of the tongue.

Something doesn't add up here.

Jake yawned and stretched. "It's been a long day. I think we should turn in." By unspoken mutual agreement, they rose and checked to make sure all of the windows and doors were locked.

CHAPTER 13

O nce again, Sally dreamed of the two wolves. This time they were on the hunt with their noses to the ground. They were joined by several other wolves that were spread out across the hills. A lone howl split the night, and they turned as one unit, racing toward the sound. They waded through a shallow creek, past a dilapidated building that may once have been a schoolhouse.

They arrived at a cave hidden by some brush halfway up a hill. Inside they found a woman's purse with the contents spread around it. The wallet lying open on the cave floor revealed a driver's license bearing the name Pamela Renee Crawford.

She bolted straight up in bed, but didn't cry out this time. Her sudden movement roused Jake. "What's going on? Are you okay? Did you have a nightmare?"

She stared at Jake for a moment and then asked, "Was Chase's mom's name Pamela Renee Crawford?"

Jake stiffened; his lips parted in surprise. "Yeah. How do you know her full name? She never told anyone her middle name."

"I had a dream about those wolves again. There were a lot of them this time. They found a cave that had her purse inside. I saw her driver's license with her full name on it." Sally's hands shook as she reached for a nearby bottle of water, taking a gulp of the cool liquid to drown the lump in her throat.

"Did you see the location of the cave?" Jake took the water bottle and set it aside. Clasping her icy hands in his warm ones, he held them to his chest.

"I don't think it was far from here. They crossed a creek to get there. The cave was hidden by some brush, but I could still hear the creek. It was a little ways up a hill, not far from an old schoolhouse." Her body sagged against him.

"I know that place. It's close to where your land joins Aunt Christie's," Chase said from his place in the doorway.

Sally jumped and squeaked. "I didn't know you were standing there! You startled me."

"Sorry about that. I wanted to make sure you were okay. Now, I want to go check the cave. If Mom's purse is there, it might give us a clue where she is."

"Chase, it was just a dream I had. It might be a wild goose chase. Besides, shouldn't the sheriff be the one to check out such things?"

"Like I told you before, your dreams are your mind's way of telling you what you need to know, Miss Sally."

"I'll call Zeke first thing in the morning and tell him we're going to check out the cave. He'll probably want to come with us. If nothing else, it will give us some exercise." Jake yawned, cracking his neck. "Knowing Zeke, he'll want to be out there early. We'd best get some more sleep."

The next morning Sheriff Zeke knocked on the door holding a tray with four small cups of coffee. "I'm glad you called me early. Let's get this show on the road. If there's something to be seen, I'd like to see it before Sunday brunch. Martha's making French Toast."

Zeke marched into the kitchen, withdrawing a map from his pocket. He smoothed the crinkled paper and pointed to various landmarks as they sipped their coffee. "We'll cross the creek here, just past the old schoolhouse," he pointed to a place on the map, "and that should put us close to the cave."

They walked out the front door to find four horses awaiting them. "I figured horses would make things a little easier. Christy loaned them to me," Zeke explained.

They mounted up, and the horses made good time. Sally had a feeling of déjà vu as they passed the old schoolhouse and crossed the creek. They moved deeper into the trees; the area too rough for even an ATV. Goose bumps raced up her arms, and the hair stood up on the back of her neck.

Zeke pulled his horse to a stop at the bottom of the hill. "Sally, where is this cave located?"

She studied the landscape and felt a pull in one direction. Dismounting her horse, she looped the reins over a nearby tree branch and began climbing the hill. All three men followed her. She stopped when she came to a thicket of brush. She studied it for a moment and then started pulling away dead overgrowth.

"Allow me," the sheriff said. "I came prepared." He stepped forward with a machete and hacked the brush to pieces in no time.

With the vines and underbrush gone, a cave entrance was revealed. Jake turned on a battery powered camping lantern and stepped inside with the sheriff. Chase and Sally followed close behind.

"The purse I saw was only a few feet inside and to the right," Sally said softly.

It was just as she had seen in her dream. Jake moved the lantern around and illuminated an old purse with lipstick, a powder compact, keys, sunglasses, and a wallet strewn around it. Chase dashed toward the wallet on the ground, but Zeke grabbed his arm before he could touch it.

"That's evidence, son," Zeke said quietly. "You can look, but don't touch."

Chase crept toward the wallet and examined it. "It's Mom's. Sally was right. That's her driver's license." He reached out, but Sally caught his arm.

"If someone's finger prints are there, you sure don't want to ruin them," she reminded him.

Zeke stepped closer. "We'll take pictures, document everything, collect the evidence, and then let the crime lab have at it. I will make sure you get everything that belonged to your mom once they're finished, Chase."

The young man studied the scene, his eyes red with unshed tears. "Thank you, Sheriff."

While Jake made a sweeping motion with the light around the cave once more, the beam revealed a sleeping bag in the corner that looked like it had never been used. Not far from it were an old bottle of wine and some candles.

Jake rubbed the back of his neck. "It looks like someone may have been planning a night of romance."

"Zeke, is that blood?" Sally pointed to a dark stain on the rock wall.

"Could be. I need to call in my detectives. Don't touch or step on anything. I'll be right back." Zeke reached for his cell phone and stepped out of the cave.

"She's dead. I'm sure of it," Chase cried in anguish.

Rushing to him, Sally hugged him tightly. "All we know for sure is that her purse is in this cave."

"Sally's right. We don't know anything more than that. At least we have a clue now. Your mama didn't run off without you. I never believed she did," Jake said, his voice full of compassion.

"The boys are on their way. I'm going to miss Sunday brunch, but this is more important. Chase, we're going to find out what happened to your mom, and I sense we're going to have answers very soon." Zeke clapped him on the shoulder.

"Thank you, sir."

"Sally, I think you and Chase should head back to the house now. Jake will be along soon. I need his help with a few things," Zeke said, tipping his hat.

"Okay. We'll see you soon," Sally replied, slipping her hand around Chase's arm.

She rode along with Chase toward the house in silence. They moved single file the same way they'd ridden in, through stands of pines, oaks, and elm trees.

CHAPTER 14

Once back at the house, Chase picked up a broom and swept the floor until there was nothing left to sweep. She watched him as she scrubbed the walls and furniture with cleaning wipes. A knock on the door made them both jump.

Chase glanced out the window and visibly relaxed. He opened the door to a petite middle-aged brunette with light brown eyes who was holding a shallow box covered by a dish towel.

"Miss Martha, it's good to see you. What brings you out this way?" He stood aside so the woman could enter the house with her burden.

"Zeke called and said you two would be here and could probably use some company. He and Jake will be along after a little while."

The woman handed the box to Chase and turned toward Sally offering her hand. "You must be Sally. I'm Zeke's wife, Martha."

Sally smiled and shook her hand. The faint scent of

lavender wafted from her skin. "It's nice to meet you. Thank you for bringing goodies. I don't have much in the way of furniture, but we can sit in the kitchen if you'd like."

Martha smiled and followed Sally into the kitchen. She settled herself at the table and withdrew a thermos from the bag on her shoulder. "Do you have mugs? I brought some hot chocolate."

Interest sparked in Chase's eyes as he rushed to the cabinet and withdrew three mugs that were part of a box of dishes Mrs. Hill had sent with Jake. He set them on the table and told the ladies, "I really love hot chocolate."

"Yes, there's something soothing about it, isn't there?" Martha asked.

Chase nodded. They were sipping their hot chocolate and getting to know each other when Jake and Zeke returned. The men joined them at the table, and Chase took two more mugs from the cabinet, filling them from the thermos.

"The evidence points toward a struggle. The detectives found some things that we missed when we first looked. We found a man's watch with a broken clasp, the heel of a woman's boot, and some other things." Zeke took a deep breath and looked sternly at Chase. "I need for you to stay away from that cave until this investigation is over. My men are still going over it. We don't want to miss anything. You understand, Chase?"

The boy looked rebellious for a moment but relented. "Yeah, I get it. I'll stay away from the cave. I want to know the minute you find my mom, though."

Zeke nodded. "Of course, you do. I'll make sure you know as soon as we find her. That's a promise. I want answers, too."

Zeke took a sip of his drink. "Martha, did you bring the French Toast?"

Martha reached into the box and withdrew an insulated

carrying bag. She unzipped it and revealed a shallow dish piled high with French Toast. She reached into her bag and grabbed a bottle of syrup and some paper plates. "Here you are, Love."

"Martha makes the best French Toast," Zeke said loading his plate.

"I don't know about that, but it fills the void," Martha said passing the dish to Sally.

They ate in silence for a while. Sally was putting her last bite in her mouth when Martha said, "That was some dream you had last night, Sally. Do you have prophetic dreams often?"

She swallowed hard, then took a sip of her hot chocolate before answering. "I've had dreams that came true before, but nothing like this. I had a dream that my husband was cheating on me once. I came home early and found him getting cozy with the cosmetics lady from down the street."

"I didn't know he cheated on you," Jake rumbled. "You said he wouldn't work, but you never mentioned he was unfaithful."

Sally shrugged. "He was a cheating bum. I don't know what else to say."

Jake slipped his arm around her and kissed her temple. "We'll talk more about this later."

"This dream about the cave was different. It was like someone was showing me a movie. I was an observer, not a participant. I watched as the wolves found the cave." Sally shook her head. "I would have dismissed it if Chase hadn't heard me telling Jake about it and insisted we investigate. I'm so glad we did."

Martha leaned into Zeke and whispered, "I think she'll do. We can always use someone with her instincts."

Sally pretended not to hear her as she puzzled the odd comment. She noticed Jake and Chase nodding at Martha in agreement.

They visited for a while longer before Martha gathered

her belongings and stood to go. "I hope to be seeing more of you, Sally. I think we'll be great friends someday."

Sally smiled. "Thank you. I enjoyed visiting with you today. Please feel free to drop by any time."

Zeke and Martha took their leave, and Sally felt lost and confused for much of the day. Midafternoon she started packing her car for the trip back home. Jake and Chase walked her to the car carrying the last of her luggage.

"Miss Sally, I know it's been a stressful weekend, but I want you to know that I appreciate your help. Your dream may lead to my mom. I can't thank you enough for that." Chase hugged her.

"I hope you find her. I hope she's okay when you do." She kissed his cheek before he turned and walked back to the house.

"Jake, is there something you want to tell me about?" Sally looked at him in question. "I feel like you have some secrets."

"Not right now, but soon." He stood a short distance away, his thumbs hooked in the front pockets of his jeans. He seemed to be struggling with inner demons. "I don't want to keep anything from you, but now isn't the time to reveal my deepest, darkest secrets. I sense you have a few of your own, as well. When things calm down, we'll have a nice long talk. Okay?"

He took one hand out of his pocket and carefully raised it, fingers spread, reaching out but not quite touching her. Her eyes tracked the movement as his hand skimmed around the side of her head, barely brushing his fingertips against her hair. A shiver rippled through her at the contact.

In a soft voice she said, "I wish I didn't have to leave."

"Then don't." The tips of his fingers trailed gently down her neck, sending heat through her. Warmth swirled in places she hadn't been touched in years.

"I have to." She tried to ignore the frantic rhythm her pulse had begun. Held captive by his intense gaze and feeling unnerved, she leaned forward.

He took her by the shoulders and brought her in for a long, passionate kiss. When he pulled away, she wanted more. She clung to his arms, corded with muscle, his skin warm beneath her fingers.

If she didn't leave now, she never would. "I've given notice. I can't just not show up," she said breathlessly.

"I'll be here when you get back. We'll start making plans for your move then. Okay?

"Yeah, okay." She slid behind the wheel and started the engine. "Have a good week, Jake."

"You, too, Sweetness. I'll be waiting here for you on Friday night."

Her mind raced with wild thoughts as she began her drive.

She wrestled with the knowledge of how her life was changing. The feel of Jake's kiss remained like an after-burn upon her lips. His touch was like those shocks of electricity she got whenever she walked over a thick carpet in socks.

Being with him gave her the sense of standing before some unopened door. Like being on the edge of an unworldly experience. More and more she found something smoldering in the smoky depths of his gaze. It both drew her to him and frightened her with its raw, naked hunger.

CHAPTER 15

Staring at the computer screen with unfocused eyes, Sally's heart wasn't in this protein shake presentation. She really didn't care if her client liked her work or not anymore. Her thoughts were centered on all of the things that she needed to do at the farm. A glance at her watch made her wonder if her house had electricity yet.

She stood, looking around to make sure no one was paying any attention to her. Walking to her office door, she closed it with a soft click. Settling back at her desk, she turned her back to her door with its tiny window, grabbed her cell phone, and dialed Jake's number before she could talk herself out of it.

The phone rang twice before he answered. "Yeah?"

"Jake, it's Sally. Did I catch you at a bad time?" She swiveled her office chair back and forth.

"Oh hi, Sweetness. No, it's not a bad time. I'm here at your place with the electric company. The tech is just packing up now. You have power."

She let out the breath she didn't even realize she was

holding. "That's great! Thank you so much for meeting them out there. Any problems?"

"Not yet. Chase will be home any minute now, and then we'll test your appliances. I already checked the pump in the well house, and it's seized up. I have a buddy coming out to look at it tomorrow. I'll let you know what he says. He'll also take samples of the water in your well and send them to the lab to make sure it's safe to drink."

She sat all the way back in her chair. "I hadn't even thought about the water being unsafe. It makes sense that it could be contaminated after all these years. Thanks for thinking of all these things."

Jake chuckled deep in his throat. "I told you there was too much city in you now. Don't worry about this stuff. I'm going to make sure your place is safe."

Sally jumped as someone rapped once on her office door and then swung it open. She dropped her cell phone in her lap and spun her head around with her most professional smile. "Yes?"

"Mr. Winston wanted me to tell you that the Sports Now people will be here for your presentation at eight o'clock in the morning." The executive's secretary spoke in clipped tones with pinched lips that made it look like it was painful to speak. Her gray hair was pulled tight in her bun, and her sensible pumps tapped the floor as if they could run away at any moment.

"Thank you, Mrs. Sours. I thought they weren't supposed to be here until next week, though."

"They moved up the meeting due to the holiday. Mr. Winston assured them it wouldn't be a problem, and you'd be ready. You will be ready, correct?" Mrs. Sours took a step closer and tried to peer at Sally's computer.

"Of course, everything will be ready for them. Thank you for the information." Sally maintained eye contact until the office busybody gave up. The secretary marched out of the office and closed the door behind her with a firm thud.

Sally retrieved her phone from her lap once she made certain no one else was close to her door. "Jake, I need to get back to work. Before I do, though, have you heard anything from Zeke?"

"The forensic lab is still going over the evidence. We won't know anything for a while. That's assuming there's anything left on those items to find."

"For Chase's sake, I sure hope we find out what happened to his mom."

"Yeah, so do I," Jake growled. "That poor kid has been through the ringer."

"Well, tell him hi for me, please. I really do need to get back to work, though. It looks like this is going to be a late night." Her fingers tightened around the phone. "Will I see you Friday night?"

"Sweetness, you will not only see me Friday night, but I will have dinner waiting for you when you get to the farmhouse." Jake heaved a loud sigh. "Just how late are you planning to work tonight? I don't like you walking out to your car alone after dark."

"I'm a big girl, and I've been walking out to my car by myself for most of my life. I will be just fine. I'll try to get out of here as early as possible, but I really need to go now." Her shoulders sagged as she stared at her computer screen.

"Okay. Be careful. I'll see you soon."

"Bye, Jake." She hit the End button on her phone and allowed herself a one-minute pity party. Then she sat up straight in her chair and focused on her presentation.

Okay, why do people love protein shakes, and why is Sports Now the best brand?

That night Sally dreamed of a huge white wolf watching over her. Instead of fearing it, she was drawn to the animal. She ran her fingers through his silky fur and reveled in the canine kisses she received in return. She snuggled into his warmth and felt safer than she had ever been in her life.

CHAPTER 16

S ally arrived at the house just as the moon rose above the eastern horizon. She dragged her luggage and a bag of household supplies through the door and was immediately enthralled by the aroma of apple pie. She stood still in the living room for a full minute just breathing it in.

"Oh good, you're here," Jake said from the open door. "Grandma brought over an apple pie, and I don't know how much longer I can keep Chase out of it."

"So that's a real pie I smell? Yay! Let's have pie!" She dropped her burden on the floor and followed her nose.

In the kitchen, she greeted Mrs. Hill with a smile and a hug. "Thank you so much for bringing pie. I've had a real hankering for apple pie since I started working on the house."

"It's my pleasure, Sally Sue. Now, I know you're going to have a busy weekend. Jake told me about all of your plans, and I wanted to be sure that you have a good meal tonight. I brought fried chicken and mashed potatoes.

Protein and veggie first, apple pie second."

Mrs. Hill ushered everyone to the table. She lifted the lids off the dishes, and Sally felt her knees go weak. The chicken was fried to crispy perfection, and the mashed potatoes were still steaming, giving off that mouthwatering aroma that you only find with perfectly mashed potatoes. No one cooked like Mrs. Hill. The only person who could ever compete was Sally's grandma.

"Of course, there's hot chocolate for everyone." Mrs. Hill smiled and winked at Chase.

"Sally, how did your shake presentation go? Did the company like your ideas?" Jake asked.

"Yes, they were happy with the new campaign I designed." She sighed. "I'm really tired of this line of work, though. I was at the office until nearly midnight, and then back by 7:30 a.m. to set up the conference room. I'm getting too old for that stuff."

Jake passed out plates, and everyone went quiet as they relished the wonderful meal. The food disappeared in record time. There wasn't even a piece of pie left.

Mrs. Hill wore a pleased grin while she cleared the table. "Thanksgiving is coming up soon. Sally, do you have any plans?"

"My plan is to come and work on the house. I have a four-day weekend because my employer gives us Black Friday off every year. I can accomplish a lot in four days."

"That's all fine and good, dear. However, I insist that you come to my house. I want all of you at my house for the noon meal on Thanksgiving. By noon meal, I mean be there by 11:00 a.m." Mrs. Hill looked each of them in the eye in turn.

"Oh, I don't want to impose. You and Jake have been way more than kind. I certainly don't want to cause you any more work," Sally protested.

"Jake, didn't you tell me that you and Sally Sue were a couple?"

"Yes, ma'am. We're a couple." Jake stretched and slipped his arm around Sally's shoulders.

"Do you really expect me to tolerate your girlfriend not celebrating Thanksgiving with us?" Mrs. Hill crossed her arms and stood her ground.

"No, ma'am. I don't expect that at all. We will all be there, Grandma. We look forward to it."

"Mrs. Hill, I appreciate the invitation, but Aunt Christy probably expects me at her house to help with the kids," Chase said.

"I've already spoken with Christy, and you're coming to my house, Chase. She has a husband who can help with the kids. They are his kids, after all. It'll be good for him to do something for once." Her eyes flashed in determination.

Chase bowed his head to Mrs. Hill. "Thank you, ma'am. I'm happy to attend. What can I bring for the meal?"

"What can we bring for the meal? Chase will be coming with me," Sally interjected.

"Well, I guess that depends on how well your stove works. A working kitchen really does make life more comfortable, Sally."

"Unfortunately, all of my appliances are toast according to Jake. I was hoping to borrow him and his truck to pick up some new ones in the morning. No one will deliver way out here." She chewed on her lip in contemplation.

"Miss Sally, not all of the appliances need replaced. Jake was able to get the well house pump and the water heater going. He said we should hear if the well water is safe to drink soon. In the meantime, it's okay to use for a shower." Chase looked at her and ducked his head. "I really like a hot shower."

She laughed, shaking her head. "Well, of course you like a hot shower. We all do. I'm excited that I won't be bathing with baby wipes this weekend. That gets old really fast."

"We can hit the appliance store first thing in the morning. I know of one that keeps everything they sell in stock, so you don't have to order it." Jake squeezed her shoulder in reassurance. "We'll make this place into a real home in no time."

"So, I gather the pipes are all okay if you're showering?" Sally asked.

"Jake fixed everything that needed fixing." Chase regarded the older man with respect shining in his gaze.

"It didn't take much. You just had a few leaks. It only took me about an hour to get them all repaired." Jake stretched his legs out in front of him and looked pleased with himself.

Mrs. Hill walked around the kitchen touching the faucet, cabinets, and counters. "Your grandma would be so proud of you for coming back and restoring this place. She truly loved this farm. I remember when your grandparents first moved here. Your dad had started his own life, and they felt like they could finally realize their dream of clean country living. I helped them put that rooster border around the kitchen." She pointed to the old peeling border with tears in her eyes.

"I'll find another rooster border, Mrs. Hill. The kitchen wouldn't be the same without it." Sally wiped a stray tear from her cheek and cleared her throat.

"I'm on Thanksgiving break next week, so I'll be able to put the border up for you if you get it this weekend. I might even be able to finish all of the repairs before you get back Wednesday evening. We're almost to the point where you'll be able to move your stuff in," Chase said.

"Wow! I wasn't expecting to be able to move in until spring. I may be able to be completely in here by Christmas at this rate." Sally laughed.

Chase looked at her from beneath his lashes, and his cheeks turned pink. "I was hoping I might be able to stay here for a while even after you get all moved in."

"I would like that, Chase. I actually need to visit with your Aunt Christy about that and some other things. You'll need a proper bed and dresser if you plan to stay here much longer. Do you know when I could catch her?"

"She's planning to stop by some time tomorrow afternoon. She said she wants to talk to you, too. She said something about making sure you two are on the same page if I'm going to be staying here."

"Would that be something that you'd like to do? Stay here with me full-time?"

The teen looked long and hard at Sally before speaking. "You could be my foster mom. Aunt Christy loves me, but she doesn't want me around. You just have to take a class and tell the foster care people that you want to be my mom. They do a background check and inspect your home. Once we get this place all fixed up, it would pass with no problem. I'm sure you would pass the class. If Aunt Christy can pass, it can't be that hard."

"Are you sure that's something you want? I've never been a mom before."

"You'd be a great mom! You treat me like my mom used to. Aunt Christy can give you all of the information."

"Okay, I'll talk to her about everything involved tomorrow. In the meantime, it's getting late, and I haven't accomplished a single thing from my to-do list tonight." Sally pushed away from the table and made her way into the living room. She was reaching for her bags when Chase scooped them up.

"I'll put these things away for you. They all go in the kitchen, right?"

Sally nodded and then noticed something was missing. "Where's my bed?" She turned in circles and peeked into the corners.

Mrs. Hill touched Sally on the shoulder. "I'm impressed with what you've accomplished here so far, dear. I can hardly wait to see this place when you're finished. But for now, I need to be going. It's getting late, and these old bones need their rest."

Sally hugged the older lady. "Thank you for everything. Dinner was delicious, and your company was much appreciated."

"Get some rest, dear. I'll see you soon." She turned and Jake walked her to her car.

CHAPTER 17

When he came back inside, Sally said, "You never answered me. Where's my bed?"

"I moved it to the bedroom. We have electricity now, which means we have heat in all of the rooms. The space heaters that your grandparents installed were all in great shape. I was shocked that they all work." Jake scratched his chin lost in his thoughts. "They shouldn't have worked at all after being unused for so long. It doesn't make much sense."

"Well, I'll take any break I can get. Buying a new stove and refrigerator is going to set me back a pretty penny. I'll bring my washer and dryer when I move in, but the other appliances will stay with my house."

"Sweetness, I'm a contractor. I don't pay full price. That means that you don't pay full price. I'm taking you to the place where I shop tomorrow. Trust me, you'll be happy with the deals." Jake kissed her forehead and took her by the hand. "Come and see your bedroom. Lights make all the difference."

Sally gasped when she saw the room. Her inflatable mattress sat with the head centered along one wall of the room beneath a brand-new ceiling fan. New burgundy curtains framed the sparkling clean window. A night stand made of repurposed pallets stood next to the bed beside an outlet that looked suspiciously new. There was even an alarm clock perched upon the pallet night stand.

"Did you have some new outlets installed? I don't remember there being one right there. Why did you install a ceiling fan? I'm never going to be able to pay you back for all of this." Sally covered her eyes with her hands.

"You aren't going to pay me back for anything. Don't you get it? You and me are meant to be together. I'm just waiting for you to move down here for good to start really spoiling you." Jake pulled her to him and crushed her lips in a quick powerful kiss.

"We haven't even discussed commitment, and now you're talking like you expect forever. I don't know. This seems too fast." Sally fought the tears threatening to overwhelm her.

"You're my soul mate." He lowered his head and hovered with his lips just a breath from her. "I was made just for you, and you were made for me. We belong together. I thought it was obvious, but I guess not. I love you, Sweetness. I always have."

"Oh Jake, I love you, too." She bit her lip in consternation. "It's just hard for me to trust. Once bitten, twice shy and all. So, we're in this for forever then? You're doing all of this because you plan to live here with me?"

"Sweetness, I won't rush you. I do plan to eventually make this our home together. You, me, and Chase will make a family. Isn't that what you want?" He watched her intently while he waited for her answer.

"I do want that." She closed the distance between them and kissed him with everything she had. She poured all of her hopes, dreams, and love into that single perfect kiss.

He pulled away and whispered, "Let me show you how much I love you."

At her nod, he crossed the room, closing and locking the bedroom door. Rushing back her, he lowered his mouth just a breath from her lips.

"Are you sure? We can wait if you have any doubts."

"I love you, and I want you, Jake." She paused, her brows furrowing. "I'm a little worried about Chase stumbling in on us, though. I don't want to scar the boy."

"Chase won't interrupt us. In fact, I'm pretty sure he will make certain we aren't disturbed. Come on, let's put that fire back into your eyes," Jake whispered huskily.

He captured her lips in a fiery kiss that scorched her all the way to her shoes. One hand tangled in her hair and tilted her head to the perfect kissing angle while the other grasped her about the waist and pulled her to him tightly. He carefully nudged her backward until she was lying on the bed. Then his lips traveled from her kiss swollen mouth across her cheek to her neck where he gently bit her.

"Oh!" she gasped, arching her neck in pleasure.

"You like that?" he growled.

"Yes," she breathed. "I like that a lot."

"Someday I plan to change your world with my bite," Jake mumbled as his fingers trailed down to the top button of her pink sweater. He slowly slipped one button free at a time. His lips followed, kissing every inch of newly exposed flesh. When all of the tiny pearl fasteners were finally released, he peeled back the sides of her shirt as though unwrapping a present.

"Oh, Sally," he groaned, "you're more beautiful than I even imagined. You're so precious. A treasure. I don't ever want to let you go." His hands roamed her contours.

"Jake," Sally panted, "I'm a precious treasure that's only half naked."

Jake's lips split in a sensuous smile. "Then let's fix that."

He carefully slid the sweater from her shoulders and down her arms until it was completely off. His lips returned to her neck, sucking hard and then gently biting down. The sensations of his touch brought a soft moan from her lips.

Passion seared through her as if her blood had turned to molten lava in her veins. She needed Jake, and she needed him now. Reaching for his shirt, she fumbled with the fabric, her fingers shaking too badly to open it.

Jake leaned back and took a long look at her, a smoldering smile on his lips before ripping his shirt off. Buttons clattered everywhere. "Better?"

She licked her lips, giving him a slight nod. With his sculpted chest finally revealed to her, she wanted to touch and taste. She tentatively ran her hands over his work-hewn muscles. A sprinkling of brown hair across his chest continued in an intriguing line down into his jeans. Her mouth watered until she finally gave in to the impulse to taste him. She ran her tongue along his collarbone and then up to his ear where she gently took his lobe into her hot mouth and flicked the tip with her tongue.

Jake growled and pushed her back down to the bed. He tugged her shoes off and dropped them to the floor. He unsnapped her jeans and pulled them along with her panties off her legs in one motion. Seeing her bared to him for the first time, his sizzling gaze roamed freely while he shucked his shoes and jeans.

Sally was thrilled to see that he wasn't wearing any underwear. She reached for him, but he caught her hands and pinned them beside her head as he loomed above her.

"Tell me what you want, Sweetness," he whispered.

"I want you to touch me," she moaned.

"As you wish," Jake murmured. "I've been waiting years for this."

Releasing her hands, he kissed her fiercely, his lips, hands, and body taking her to heights she never dreamed of reaching. Each touch left a trail of fire across her skin. He worshipped her as if she were the most precious thing in the universe.

She cried out in ecstasy. She would never get enough of this man. Barely had this thought crossed her mind when he howled long and loud with his own release, sounding for all the world like a proud alpha wolf.

They lay wrapped together in bliss for a few minutes before Jake lifted his head from her chest to gaze into her eyes. "You're mine, now. You understand that, don't you, Sally? I'm not giving you up now."

"Yes, I'm yours, Jake. And you are mine. That was the most incredible experience of my life."

They basked in their afterglow together, half asleep, for a long while before Jake stirred. He looked deeply into her eyes.

"We have some things to talk about. I don't want secrets between us. I need to explain something, but I think it would be best to show you instead of just tell you. We need to get dressed and go find Chase."

CHAPTER 18

"Chase, can you come here, please?" Jake called. A moment later, he appeared in the doorway. "What's up? Is everything okay?"

"I'm going to explain everything to Sally. I'm going to show her the other part of myself. I thought maybe you might want to join us for that conversation."

Chase stood staring at them for a few heartbeats, then moved farther into the room before he spoke. "What would you like for me to do, Jake?"

"Just keep her company if you would, please. She may need some emotional support." Jake looked dead serious.

"Whatever it is you have to tell me, it can't be so bad that I would need someone to comfort me. This is silly. Just tell me already." Sally shook her head at his foolishness.

"Let's go into the living room where there's more open space." Jake took her hand and led her into the front room. His spine was straight and his pace measured, full of purpose.

"Sally, it's very important that you tell no one, no matter what you think of what I'm about to you show you. Many lives rely on this secret being kept hidden. I need your word of honor." Jake regarded her with solemn eyes.

"Yes, of course. You have my word that whatever I'm about to see will remain a secret. I won't tell anyone."

"I'm only showing you because you're my mate, and it's time for me to treat you as such. It's not fair to keep this from you if I expect you to give me your heart."

Jake backed away a few steps and took off his clothes. He stood before them in all of his naked glory. Just as Sally was about to say something, he blew her a kiss. Then his body twisted and contorted. One moment he was a man and the next he had morphed into a huge white wolf.

"Jake?" Sally took a tentative step closer to him. "Is that really you?"

The wolf closed the distance between them and gently licked her hand. She touched the top of his head and stroked his soft fur.

"You're beautiful. Just like in my dream. But wait. There were two." She turned to Chase who had gone pale.

"Are you the black wolf from my dream, Chase? I dreamed of a white one and a black one. They work together in my dreams."

Jake the wolf yipped at Chase.

"It's okay, Jake. If I want Miss Sally to be my foster mom, then it's only right she knows about me, too."

Jake yipped again and started pacing around the room.

Sally looked over at Chase just in time to see him turn his back to her, shuck out of his clothes, and morph into a giant black wolf. Both wolves nudged her with their noses. They licked her face and rubbed all over her. "Yes, I see. You're both beautiful wolves," she said as she buried her fingers in their soft fur. "I sure am glad you're on my side."

Both wolves threw their heads back and howled long and loud. They sat there like that for a little while before morphing back into the men that Sally had come to know and love. They were naked as the day they were born and completely comfortable in their skin. They casually got dressed as if having someone watch them was the most natural thing in the world.

They stared at each other for a few minutes before Sally couldn't take the silence anymore. "How did you two become what you are? Were you born that way? Were you bitten? How?"

Jake answered first. "We were both bitten by the same lone wolf. It happened a short time after Chase's dad went to jail. The guy came around claiming that Tony owed him money. He obviously couldn't get it from Tony, so he tried to get it from Chase."

"I had no money to give him, so you could say he decided to take a pound of flesh. He beat the tar out of me. Jake came along and saw what was happening. He jumped right into the fight. We both ended up bit, and the guy took off. I don't think he meant to bite us. It was just an instinct during the fight. Luckily, there's an alpha in the area who sensed what happened and came to investigate. He took us home with him for the night and explained everything." Chase's eyes gleamed at the memory.

"We didn't change until the first full moon after we were bitten. The alpha was there to make sure we didn't panic and knew what to do. After that first change, he taught us control. We don't need the full moon to change, but the urge is stronger to do so during that lunar phase. We can change at will, as you saw tonight."

"Can all werewolves change at will?" she asked calmly.

Jake watched her closely as he answered. "No. Most only change with the full moon. Only a few of us can control it. Our alpha told us he thinks it comes from a few werewolves who were exposed to a chemical of some sort during World War II. Everyone born or turned from those men have possessed the ability to control the shift. We think he's a descendent of one of those men."

"So, even though you didn't ask for this, I guess you guys lucked out."

Jake slowly approached her and took her hands in his. "I can't help but notice that you're taking the werewolf thing very well. You don't seem that surprised."

"Yeah, I was really worried about you finding out." Chase came up behind her and touched her shoulder.

"I already suspected it. Something deep inside me knew. I kept having those wolf dreams. I even had them when I was at home in my own bed, far away from the woods. I kept telling myself that it was impossible, but my subconscious already knew. It's like you said, Chase, dreams are our mind's way of telling us something we need to know." Sally wrapped her arms around both men. "I have my very own set of werewolves. How did I get so lucky?"

"We're the ones who are lucky, Miss Sally. This is something that most people don't accept that great."

"Wait, is that why your uncle gives you such a hard time, Chase? Because he refuses to accept this part of you?" Sally broke away from them to pace the room.

Chase sat down on the floor and looked up at her. "Uncle Ray doesn't know. I told Aunt Christy, but she's the only one of my family who knows my secret. Uncle Ray hates me for moving into his house and eating his food. He hates me because Aunt Christy loves me. He hates me because I don't have parents. He hates me because Danny convinced him that I'm no good. If he knew I was a werewolf, he'd try to kill me."

"I would really like to punch your Uncle Ray in the face," Sally seethed.

Jake smiled like the predator he was. "That's my girl. You've got just enough ferocity to be my perfect mate. Don't worry, one of these days Ray will get what's coming to him. We all do, one way or another."

Sally sank to her knees and wrapped her arms around Chase's shoulders. "You are a wonderful young man, and I'm glad to have you in my life. I couldn't choose a better son even if I was given the chance."

Chase looked deep into her eyes and proclaimed, "Mom would have absolutely loved you. I know if she had to choose who would raise me, she would have picked you." He gave her a fierce hug, sprang to his feet, and sprinted to his room.

Jake helped Sally to her feet. He kissed her cheek and whispered, "That is the highest compliment that boy could ever give you."

A few tears escaped her control before she answered. "I really hope we find his mom running around with a horrible case of amnesia and can reunite them."

"We should have a forensic report soon. It doesn't look good. The odds of Pam being alive are real slim." Jake shook his head. "I just can't figure out who would have taken her. I don't believe for a minute that she ran off with someone."

"Would the DNA still be viable after so long? There was blood in the cave. If it belonged to her kidnapper, would the police be able to use it to find him?"

"Those are great questions for Zeke. It depends on how well preserved it was. You should ask him about it the next time you see him. I'm no scientist. I build houses for a living, remember?"

Sally grinned. "Yeah, you build houses instead of blowing them down. The irony isn't lost on me."

"So, you think I'm the big bad wolf? Let me show you a thing or two about being bad with a wolf." Jake scooped her up and carried into the bedroom. He kicked the door shut and stretched her out on the bed. "I'm going to huff and puff and blow your clothes off."

"Silly, wolf. Stop blowing and going, and just come to bed."

"Silly? I think I need to demonstrate exactly how serious a wolf I am," Jake growled just before he leapt on top of her.

She giggled as his lips found her neck. He sprinkled butterfly kisses up the side of her neck, over her jaw, and the tip of her nose. Then he found that special spot behind her ear, and she was lost in the moment.

"I'm serious about making you happy." He ran his teeth along her collarbone. "I'm serious about creating a life with you." He licked her ear. "I'm serious about bringing you the most pleasure you've ever known."

Captivated by his intense gaze, she realized she'd been holding her breath as her heartbeat thundered in her ears. Arched beneath him, she panted, "Okay, I believe you. You are a very serious wolf."

He ran his index finger over her chin and looked deep into her eyes. "Sweetness, I am nothing but serious about you. About us. You got away once. You left a hole in my heart the size of Montana. Now that you're back, I'm never letting you go. Please tell me you feel the same way."

She smiled at the love shining in his eyes. "I never forgot you. Coming back here is the best thing I've ever done if for no other reason than I found you waiting for me. I love you. I never want to be without you again."

He closed the distance between them, and they took each other to new heights of passion that neither had ever believed possible. When they had banked their fires for the night, they lay entwined and basked in the glow of their growing bond.

CHAPTER 19

Sally awakened early, rolled over and looked out the window. The sun bathed the treetops with light, turning them into a blaze of gold. Even though some people might think her foolish for coming back, she loved this land where her grandparents had created a loving home.

She enjoyed a long hot shower before starting her day, thinking about all of the things she needed to accomplish before she went back home. Dressed in a pair of jeans and purple flannel shirt, she put on thick socks and athletic shoes before leaving the room.

In the kitchen, she set out breakfast bars for what she hoped was the last time. A stove and refrigerator would make so much difference. She'd be able to scramble a dozen eggs tomorrow morning.

Jake stumbled to the coffee pot with serious bed head. "Good morning, Sweetness."

Sally accepted his kiss on the cheek with a small grin. "Good morning, Big Bad Wolf. How did you sleep?"

"I slept real good because I had you to keep me warm. Then you had to go and get up. I got cold in the bed by myself." He stuck his bottom lip out in an exaggerated pout.

"We need to get an early start. I'd like to get to town and then be back home and have the appliances installed by noon. So, you better hurry and shower."

She was about to open a breakfast bar when Jake grasped her wrist. "We'll get something in town. Wolves need lots of protein. A processed carb bar just won't cut it."

She looked at the bar in disgust, and tossed it back on the table. "Should we wake Chase up and take him with us?"

"Yeah, a change of scenery might do the boy a world of good. He doesn't get out much." Jake tucked a stray lock of hair behind her ear. "You're a kind person for thinking to include him."

"He's a good young man. He deserves every kindness. I'll wake him while you shower. Now scoot." She swatted Jake on the rear as he headed toward the tiny bathroom.

"Don't be starting something you can't finish, Sweetness." His lips quirked up at the edges in a sexy smile.

Sally walked over to the back-bedroom door and knocked. "Chase, would you like to go to town with Jake and me? We're going out for breakfast and then to the appliance store."

Silence greeted her query. "Chase? Are you in there?" She pushed the door open to reveal an empty sleeping bag. "Where could he have gone?"

"I just went out to get some pears off the tree in the back yard." The boy's voice came from right behind her.

She yelped and spun to face him. "Don't scare me like that!"

Chase hung his head and slumped his shoulders. "I'm sorry, Miss Sally. I didn't mean to scare you."

Tears sprang to her eyes at his crestfallen expression, and she wrapped her arms around his waist in a firm hug. "You aren't in trouble. Don't you dare feel bad. You just startled me. That's all. I was worried about you. You move around here like a ninja or something."

"You said you were looking for me. What did you need?"

"Would you like to go into town with Jake and me today? We're going to have breakfast someplace and then head to the appliance store. We thought you might enjoy the outing." She couldn't hide her big smile when his eyes widened in surprise.

"Yes, ma'am. That would be great. It's been a real long time since I went anywhere but school, work, and church."

"It's settled then. You can shower as soon as Jake finishes and then we'll go."

"I actually showered last night while you and Jake were uh . . . going to sleep." His cheeks turned pink and he refused to meet her gaze.

"Chase, does it bother you when Jake and I go to sleep together?"

"No. Mating is the most natural thing in the world. I just don't want to interrupt. Uncle Ray always got real mad if anyone made any noise in the house when he and Aunt Christy . . . you know."

Sally took Chase by the shoulders. "Ray isn't here. Jake and I know that you're in the house with us. We want you here. You won't upset us by making a normal amount of noise. You can even watch TV once I get one moved down here."

"Thank you. I'll enjoy that. I don't get to watch much TV at Aunt Christy's house." He laughed. "I think I'd like to watch one of them game shows. They look fun, but Ray hates them."

"Once we get a TV hooked up, I'll introduce you to a few of my favorites. I think you'd enjoy the word puzzle one. I grew up watching it every night." A smile tugged her lips at the memory.

"I'll go put some better clothes on and be back in a minute." Chase bounded to his room with a spring in his step and returned two minutes later.

Jake emerged from the bathroom with damp hair and smelling like a piece of rainforest heaven. He looked from Sally to Chase and smiled broadly. "Well, what are you standing around here for? Let's go!"

They all piled into Jake's extended cab truck and headed for the nearest sizable city, which was roughly a half hour away. They had driven a few miles when Sally asked, "Where are we having breakfast?"

Jake glanced at Chase who had been watching the passing landscape out the window. "Is there any place in particular that you'd like to eat? What are you hungry for?"

"I don't know. I can eat pretty much anything. Wherever you and Miss Sally want to go is just fine with me." Chase returned to looking out the window.

"Sweetness?"

"Is Ma's Diner still around? Grandma used to take me there every once in a while. They had amazing skillet breakfasts from what I remember." She sat back in her seat completely content for the first time in many years.

"Ma's Diner it is, then." Jake grinned. "You'll like it, Chase. They have steak so fresh you can practically hear it moo."

"Steak for breakfast? That sounds amazing!" Chase leaned forward with a big smile. "I've never had steak for breakfast."

Jake glanced at Chase with a frown. "Your body needs steak and eggs every once in a while. It gives you lots of energy and will help you gain strength. Meat is important."

The rest of the drive was spent in relative silence. When Jake pulled into the parking lot of Ma's Diner, both Sally and Chase came to attention. The flat-roofed red brick building was small and screamed early twentieth century architecture, but it was the sign in the window that caught Sally's eye.

"If Ma Don't Have It, You Don't Need It," she read aloud. "That's an interesting slogan. I don't remember that from when I was a kid."

Jake's eyes gleamed and his lips widened into a gleeful smile. "It's a fairly new addition. Ma got tired of the young folks trying to order fancy coffee. Hers is the best because it's strong, rich, and fragrant. She has cream and sweetener on each table, but you won't catch her serving anything but black coffee. You're in for a treat, Sweet Sally Sue."

CHAPTER 20

Chase and Sally walked in first and were greeted by Ma, herself. "Hi! Welcome to Ma's Diner. I'm Ma," announced the plump woman with gray curls framing her round pink face.

"Ma, it sure smells great in here," Jake said from behind Chase.

"Jake? Well, tarnation, get over here and give me a hug!"

He stepped forward, and Ma grabbed him by the shoulders, squeezing like she thought he would blow away. "I haven't seen you in forever and a day! Where ya been?"

"I've been helping Sally Sue here get her grandparents' farmhouse ready for her to move into. You remember Sally, right? She's Fern's granddaughter."

"As I live and breathe! I ain't seen you since you was knee high to a grasshopper. Get over here and give Ma a hug!"

Sally stepped forward and suddenly found herself enveloped in Ma's tight embrace.

"Wasn't right what happened with that place. Wasn't right at all." Ma put her hands on her hips and regarded Sally. "Did that weasel finally give you the place after all?"

"No. I bought it at a tax sale. Danny failed to pay the taxes for several years. He's not happy that I bought it." Sally shook her head. "I don't get it. You'd think he'd be happy to get out from under the responsibility. I'm going to turn it back into a profitable operation." She kept her doubts and moments of panic to herself.

"That boy ain't never gonna be happy 'bout nothin'. You can take that to the bank." Ma cocked her head to the side. "You grew up right nice even if you were cheated. Good job, honey."

"You say that like you know something. Do you know why Uncle Frank inherited the farm instead of Dad? All the lawyer would tell us was that Grandma and Grandpa wanted Uncle Frank to have it."

"Well, that's a long story. Let's get ya'll seated and yer breakfast started. Then I'll come out and visit."

Ma seated them next to a large window with a view of the parking lot. "Best seats in the house." She laughed at her own joke. "People don't come to Ma's Diner for the atmosphere. They come here for downhome cooking. Now what can I get ya?"

Jake spoke first. "I'll have the steak and eggs platter, and make that steak rare, please. I'd also like a cup of your amazing coffee."

Ma laughed loud and long. "Honey, it will still be mooing when I bring it out."

Chase looked up shyly. "I'll have what he's having, but I don't want coffee. What else do you have?"

"We have apple juice, orange juice, tea, and pop. I think you might enjoy our hot chocolate, though. Am I right?"

Chase perked up. "Yes, ma'am. I would love some hot chocolate. How did you know?"

"I know a lot about a lot of things. Ya look like a hot

chocolate kind of guy." Ma winked at him and then turned to Sally.

"I'd like pancakes and fried eggs, over easy. I'd love a cup of your wonderful coffee. Jake was telling me about it on the drive here."

Ma smirked. "Would you like your pancakes buttered with your eggs on top?"

Sally was transported back to her childhood remembering that's exactly how her grandma had made pancakes and eggs. "Yes, please. And Ma? Thank you."

"Your granny and me grew up together. We were good friends. She loaned me some of the money to start this place. She let me pay her $20.00 a week until I was able to turn a profit and repay her proper. The least I can do is take care of her precious Bunny."

Sally sat back in surprise. "Bunny? Grandma used to call me that when I was a little girl. I guess you knew her pretty well."

"Like I said, we were good friends. She always swore you were the smartest kid she'd ever seen. Maybe she was right." Ma patted her shoulder and took their order to the kitchen.

"Ma's interesting. I didn't realize someone here would know so much about my life." Sally rubbed her forehead. "I don't know if that's a good thing or a bad thing."

"She means well, and you may learn something by talking to her. Ma is about as country as you can get. She wanted to open Ma's Diner in Elderberry, but Frank blocked her. He was on the city council and refused to grant her the permits she needed. That's why she opened the diner here. Nobody in River Falls cared who she might be friends with or what she knew. They just wanted to be sure the place was safe and passed all of the inspections."

"Why would Uncle Frank block permits for a diner? That's bizarre."

"Frank and me dated in high school." Ma spoke and set

drinks down in front of them, slipping into the booth beside Chase. "Too full of himself for my taste, so the relationship didn't go very far. He was none too happy to be dumped. I think I'm the only one who ever did that to him." Ma shrugged her shoulders. "He probably hated me until his dying day, but that was his problem."

"Ma, what do you know about Uncle Frank inheriting the farm?" Sally leaned closer and propped her chin on her fist.

"I think your grandparents were hoodwinked. There's no way they would willingly leave that place to a money grubber like Frank." Ma snorted. "George didn't do nothing to deserve being cut out of the will. Fern and Dale loved him dearly and just plain adored you."

"You think they were coerced?" Sally asked.

"Well, something was fishy as all get out with that will." Ma shook her head sadly. "Something was fishy about the car accident that killed them, too, if you ask me."

"I thought it was a freak accident. No one ever said anything about foul play." Sally shivered and crossed her arms in front of her.

Jake slipped his arm around her shoulders and drew her back into his embrace, snuggling her tightly into his side.

"Dale was a good driver. He wasn't one to speed down the road. He always took his time. No. I'll never believe that he fell asleep at the wheel and drove them off the side of that mountain. Accident, my fanny!"

"Did the accident happen late at night?" Jake asked.

"No. It happened at two o'clock in the afternoon on a beautiful spring day. It wasn't even raining." Ma shook her head. "No, somethin' bad happened to them. Nobody will ever convince me otherwise."

Sally was quiet for a moment, her brow pulled into a frown. "So, you think Grandma and Grandpa were murdered? Did you tell the police what you thought?"

"Yeah, but they weren't interested in hearing from me.

Told me they had a closed case. It was an accident and that's that."

Chase looked at Ma with an eyebrow quirked. "What do you think happened with the will? Do you think Frank strong armed them?"

"No. Dale wasn't the type of man to be pushed around. More like the papers were switched on him when he signed them or something. Frank was devious enough to pull something like that."

"Why would he do that, though? He just let the place sit vacant for all these years." Sally's voice was thick with unshed tears.

"Maybe Dale knew something that Frank didn't want to get out." Ma held her gaze. "They weren't that close anyways."

"What? I never heard that. It really doesn't make sense." Sally thought for a minute. "Now that you mention it, Danny did tell me that there was a reason Dad was written out of the will. So, he must know something."

Chase snorted. "Yeah, well good luck getting him to tell you anything. He just goes around spreading lies all the time."

Ma chuckled. "What does Dummy Danny even do for a living these days? I can't imagine he wields any sort of power."

Chase huffed a frustrated breath. "He's a car salesman at Honest Abe's Used Cars. I don't know how anyone could possibly trust a word he says."

Ma nodded. "Are he and the mayor's daughter still an item?"

Sally said, "I didn't realize he was seeing the mayor's daughter. That could explain why some people think he's credible."

Jake squeezed Sally tighter to him. "Danny and Chloe have been on again off again since high school. You'd think she'd get smart and move on after all these years. If he hasn't proposed yet, he never will."

"No way would I stick with a guy for that long who wasn't serious." Sally looked Jake straight in the eye.

"I already told you that I'm serious." He leaned over and kissed the tip of her nose. "I believe we established that last night."

"So we did." She could feel the heat fill her cheeks and knew she was blushing.

"Oh, here comes your food," Ma said rising from the table. "I'll let ya'll eat in peace. You know where to find me if you want to talk some more." She turned to Sally. "Be careful, Bunny. There are things out there that can get ya."

They all enjoyed their breakfast and moved on to more pleasant topics of conversation. "Chase, how's your steak?" Sally couldn't resist asking as she watched him wolf it down.

He looked up with pink cheeks. "It's real good. Probably the best steak I've ever had." Then he grinned. "Do you think Ma would teach me to cook like this?"

Jake smiled indulgently. "Maybe. We'll ask her next time we come. We need to hurry and eat so we can get to the appliance store. We still have a lot to do before Sally meets with Christy this afternoon."

"Yes, and I want a working refrigerator by the end of the day, if nothing else. I can live without the stove for a while longer, but I'm tired of eating out of an ice chest."

They finished their meals and went to the antique cash register to pay. Ma met them at the counter. "Everything to your liking?"

"It was delicious as always, Ma. We'll be back soon. Chase, here, had never eaten steak for breakfast before."

Ma looked over her half rim glasses at the young man. "You're kidding. A young man like you needs to eat a lot of meat to stay healthy. You come back soon and old Ma will fix you up with the biggest steak in my kitchen."

"Could I watch you cook it? I'd like to learn how." Chase looked at her with hope filling his eyes.

"You bet your bippy you can watch me cook your steak. I may just teach ya a few more things, too. Come back soon."

CHAPTER 21

The contractor supply store was busy with a bustling crowd. Jake expertly led Sally through the aisles to the appliances she needed. She realized from the price tags that his cost wasn't even close to what the same items were in a regular store.

"Wow. With these prices, I can afford a stove, fridge, and a microwave. That'll be really nice. We can have microwave popcorn and frozen burritos. Oh, it's going to be glorious!" Sally clapped her hands together.

Jake stared at her for a moment. "Popcorn and frozen burritos excite you? You really are my mate. I eat them together a lot."

"Me, too!" She beamed a huge smile. "We really do have a lot in common, don't we?"

They purchased a refrigerator, stove, microwave, and a stand mixer. It wasn't until they got to the cash register that there was a problem. "Sally, I have to pay. Your money is no good here because you aren't a contractor."

"Then I will pay you back for them. I don't care what

you say; I'm not letting you pay for all of this out of your pocket."

Jake heaved a giant sigh. "Yeah, sure. You can pay me back. We'll talk about it later."

Feeling like she won an argument, Sally smiled and directed the employees pushing appliance carts out to Jake's truck.

She'd just overseen the careful loading of each appliance when the two men in her life joined her. She smiled brightly and asked, "Who wants ice cream?"

Chase shifted his weight from one foot to the other and stared at the ground. When he finally looked up, he gave her a shy smile "Ice cream would be okay. You know, if you want some."

Sally grinned and said, "Okay. We'll make a quick stop at the grocery store and then we're off to find some dessert."

Sally was glowing with contentment when they arrived back at the farmhouse, still sipping their shakes. The sun shone brightly from its zenith, and they would soon have the ability to store and prepare food. Life looked better with each passing day.

"Chase and I will unload the appliances if you want to carry the groceries in. We'll have these set up in no time." Jake's face was alive with happiness.

"That sounds like a deal to me." Sally grabbed all of the grocery bags and lugged them into the house. She opened the door just as the guys reached it with the refrigerator. She held it wide, and they easily maneuvered the fridge into place. Jake plugged it in, and they repeated the process with the stove.

They found Sally happy dancing in the kitchen when they returned with the microwave and stand mixer. "I've never seen anyone so happy with kitchen appliances before," Chase said as he set the mixer on the counter. "Do you just love to cook or something?"

She laughed. "I don't mind it, but it's not something I love to do. I'm just happy to be able to cook any time I want. We're going to have a hot lunch today! Isn't that exciting? I'll even let you pick. Do you want beef burritos or chicken pot pie?"

Chase smiled at the woman he wanted as a mom. "Beef burritos sound good to me. Did you get any hot chocolate?"

"Yes, I bought some. It won't take any time at all to make in the microwave. So, what's with you and hot chocolate, anyway?"

"All of the werewolves I know love hot chocolate. I can't get enough of it. I'd rather have hot chocolate over a pop any day." Chase nodded thoughtfully. "Maybe that's what sets us apart from a common canine. Chocolate is really bad for dogs, but werewolves crave it."

Sally nodded. "That's interesting. I've seen you drink very little else. I'll be sure to buy it in bulk for you."

He stared at her for a moment before giving her a quick hug. "I'd like that. Thanks."

She laughed indulgently and patted his back. "It's not a big deal, sweetie. Really, I can afford it."

"It's the fact that you're willing to do that for me that makes you the best."

"What's all this?" Jake asked leaning on the doorjamb.

"Miss Sally is going to buy me hot chocolate." Chase turned and abruptly ran to his room.

She stared after him for a few moments before turning to Jake. "What the heck happened? He was all happy one minute and then running off the next."

Jake ambled to the kitchen table and sat down. He pulled out a chair and motioned for Sally to join him.

"Chase has had a hard go of it since his mom disappeared. Don't get me wrong – Christy loves that boy. She has a hard time showing it because Ray has a fit every time she does the slightest thing for him. Add to that the fact that Danny pretty much turned the whole community against him, and it chips away at his self-esteem. Chase doesn't think he's worth anything. I've been trying to change that. He has those teen hormones rushing through him all the time, so he's always second guessing himself. With you here, I think he's starting to see some of his own value, but he's afraid to believe it."

Sally wiped a stray tear from her cheek. "That poor kid. I can't imagine what he's been through. And it's not over yet. We still don't know what happened to Pam. I have a feeling that he is going to have a lot more heartache before it's all over."

Jake touched her chin and made her look at him. "He has you in his court now. He's going to come out of this okay as long as he has you."

Sally gave him a watery smile and stood. "Okay, enough mushy stuff. Let's cook some burritos. I want to bake them in the oven and then top them with cheese. Do you like chili on your burritos? I have time to whip up a quick batch while the burritos are baking."

He looked at her with mock gravity. "We do not have time to make good chili. You know as well as I do that chili needs to simmer for a few hours before the flavors marry properly."

She laughed. "I suppose you're right. How many do you want?"

"Better cook all eight. I'm hungry."

She shrugged and preheated the oven. When the burritos were done, she topped them with cheese and set the table. She popped a bag of microwave popcorn and poured the contents into a large bowl. She opened a package of peanut butter cookies and placed them in the center of the table. Chase's eyes widened when he walked back into the room.

"Miss Sally, you bought me cookies." His lips turned up in a small smile.

"Of course. Did you think I'd forget them?"

"Ice cream and peanut butter cookies in the same day.

Steak for breakfast. You are an angel, Miss Sally."

She smiled and said, "Now that we have an oven, I can make cookies as often as you want."

They sat and ate together. "Jake, you were right. We did need the whole package of burritos." Sally stared at the empty serving plate in wonder.

"Yeah, I'm pretty wise about some things." Jake grinned wickedly. "Like the way I knew you were mine the minute I saw you standing in Grandma's living room trying to buy fire wood." He chuckled. "Then I had to chase you down in a thunderstorm to make you see reason. You had me nervous for a minute."

CHAPTER 22

Aknock on the front door startled them. "That's Aunt Christy. I'll get it," Chase said rushing to the door.

He returned a few moments later with a petite woman who had gray-streaked black hair and fine worry lines around her eyes. Behind her glasses, her nut-brown eyes had a light to them, illuminated by everything that went on in her sharp mind. Her naturally dark skin was rough from too much sun and made her look older than Sally knew her to be. Her red turtleneck, which still bore her nametag from the bank where she worked, was tucked into her black slacks, evidence that she had just gotten off work.

She smiled when she saw Sally and extended her hand. "I'm Christy. We used to go to Sunday school together when we were little. I really appreciate you taking such great care of Chase."

Sally accepted the offered hand and shook it firmly. "I'm Sally. I remember you. Chase is a good kid. It's been my pleasure. He's really helped me more than I've helped him, though. He's a talented handy man. He also has an amazing protective instinct."

Christy patted Chase's arm and smiled proudly. "Yes, he does. I'm glad he could help you."

Chase ducked his head. "Well, I'll let you ladies talk. Jake, what project should we tackle next?"

"Let's go take a look at that south wall again. Then we can run up the hill and get the mail. We may have the water results by now." The men left the room planning the rest of their day.

"So, Christy, would you like something to drink? I have bottled water, pop, coffee, and I can make some tea. We just bought appliances today, so I'm excited to actually have food and drink like a normal person."

"A regular pop if you have it would be great. I don't get to indulge very often. Ray thinks I'm getting too chunky." Christy patted her behind self-consciously.

"Don't listen to him. I think you look great. When a woman reaches our age, she supposed to have a little padding back there." She grabbed a glass and filled it with ice from the bag she bought in town and poured a tall glass full of cola.

Christy laughed. "I can see why Chase loves you so much." She looked around the kitchen curiously. "This is sure coming along nicely. I came to check on Chase a couple weeks ago, and this doesn't even look like the same kitchen."

"Thanks. Now that we have power, everything should go pretty quick." She set the glass down in front of Christy and claimed a seat across the table from her. "You aren't here to talk about my kitchen, though, are you?"

Christy laughed. "You're right." She looked Sally straight in the eye. "I love that kid with all my heart. What he has been through tears at my soul. I want to hug him to me and never let him go. But Ray absolutely hates him. He's always after me to call the foster care people and have him removed from our house. He's my blood. I can't do that. I won't do that. Please tell me that you understand."

"Of course, I understand. I also want to grab the kid and protect him from the world. He's in that weird place in life where he still needs that to a certain degree, and then he also needs to tests his wings a little."

Christy nodded. "Staying here and working on your house has done wonders for his self-esteem. He walks taller, speaks with more certainty, and doesn't second guess his decisions nearly so much. And he loves you. I can't tell you how special that is. He told me that he wants you to be his mom."

Sally's eyes filled with tears, and a few broke loose before she could stop them. "Yes, we've discussed it a little. Is that something that you would be okay with? Keep in mind that I have zero experience in raising kids."

Christy reached across the table and grabbed Sally's hand. "He told me that if he was to choose one person in the world to be his mom besides my sister, it would be you. You're doing something right. My boy is stronger, more confident, and he's even doing better in school. I got a call from his history teacher last week asking me if we were trying new study tactics because he made a perfect score on his last test. Sally, he hasn't scored well on a test since Pam went missing. This is huge." She released Sally's hand and took a gulp of her pop.

"He didn't mention any test to me, but I'm glad he did well. He's a smart kid. I imagine he's had plenty of time to study while staying here. There's pretty much nothing else to do."

"It's more than a nothing else to do thing. He's always complained about his homework and studying before. He was more interested in getting my kids ready for bed than his studies. Anything to put off his schoolwork." Christy shook her head. "No, you've done something to him. Something special. He's responding to you in a way he never has to me."

"I don't know what I've done that's so special."

"He told me about your dream. The one that led you to Pam's purse. I think you may be a gift to Chase from God. You were here a few days and made a breakthrough on her case that no one else had been able to come near in the six years since she disappeared. He said you led them right to the cave." She started to sniffle, so Sally got up and grabbed a box of tissues, placing it on the table between them. "No, I was wrong. You're not a gift to Chase. You're a gift to us all."

"I'm sorry, Christy. I can't imagine what you've been through. Losing your sister, trying to raise your nephew, and keeping your own family together can't be easy."

"I'm happy to care for Chase. I just have all these obstacles thrust in front of me time after time. I don't understand why people are so mean to the boy. He has a heart of pure gold, you know."

"Yes, I can attest to that. He's a very kind young man. You've done a good job with him. Don't ever doubt that." Sally took a tissue and dabbed at her own eyes.

"So, that brings us to the reason for my visit. I'm Chase's foster mother as well as his aunt. The state insisted he go into foster care, so I took the class and jumped through their hoops to keep him with me. He's family, as I said before."

"Of course," Sally agreed. "I would have done the same thing."

"So, as a foster child, the state pays for his medical care and whatnot. They also send me a maintenance check every month. It's not a whole lot, a little over $300.00, but it helps. I want you to have the money for this month since he's been staying here." She pulled a wad of cash from her back pocket.

"Christy, I can't accept any money for letting Chase stay here. He's been working. He earned his room here. No, that wouldn't be right at all." Sally shook her head and scooted her chair back a few inches.

"I was expecting you to say that. So, here's another proposal. Take the money and buy Chase some microwavable food, maybe some hot chocolate, and for the love of all that is good, please get the boy some peanut butter cookies. My daughter, Alice, is allergic to peanuts, so Chase doesn't get to have anything with peanut butter in it at my house."

Sally laughed. "I bought him some today. He ate the whole package after he wolfed down three burritos smothered in cheese."

"Yeah, our boy can put away the food." Christy sighed. "I know you aren't ready to move here full time yet, but I'd really like for you to become his official guardian when you do."

"Why are you so anxious to transfer guardianship?"

Christy took a deep breath. "No one knows this, but me. You can't say a word to anyone. Please promise me."

"I'm really good at keeping secrets, Christy. I've been hit with a humdinger already this weekend."

"Chase told me he showed you his wolf. He's beautiful, isn't he?"

"Gorgeous, but I don't think that's the secret you were referring to," Sally said.

"If Pam is pronounced dead, it's vitally important that I not be Chase's guardian," Christy said in a rush.

Sally's brows furrowed in confusion. "Why not?"

Christy leaned closer, the faint scent of vanilla wafting from her, and whispered, "Pam has a sizeable life insurance policy. I've been keeping up the payments. If Chase is under age when she's pronounced dead, the guardian gains stewardship of the money. I'm married to Ray, which means he has access to all of my accounts. He has a terrible gambling problem. He would blow through the money so fast that there wouldn't be anything left by the time Chase reaches adulthood."

Sally sat back in her chair. "So, you believe she's dead, then?"

Tears flowed down Christy's cheeks. "Pam would never have abandoned her child. She's lying dead in a ditch or hole somewhere. I can feel it. I just don't understand why the sheriff didn't investigate further when she first disappeared."

"Chase tells me that Zeke wasn't the sheriff then. Who was?"

"Old Hank Meriwether was sheriff then. You may remember him. He was good buddies with your Uncle Frank."

Sally studied Christy as another puzzle piece clicked into place. "That's an interesting coincidence."

"Yeah, I always thought it was fishy." Christy gulped the rest of her pop. "So, you understand why I want someone who has Chase's best interests at heart to be his guardian, right?"

Sally nodded. "Of course. I'm honored that you would choose me. Chase said there's a class I need to take. Can you send me some information about it?"

Christy smiled brightly. "Yes. I have a packet in the car." She stood and grabbed her purse. "If you'll walk me out, I'll give it to you."

"Chase needs a bed and dresser. Does he have his own or should I buy them for him?"

"He has a storage building full of furniture. The bank took the house back, but I put all of the stuff from Pam's house in a storage locker. I pay for the storage fee and the life insurance policy out of the money I earn by cleaning houses in River Falls for cash after work. Ray thinks I'm going to Bible study. That's the cleverest lie I've ever told."

"You are a smart cookie," Sally said walking to the door. "When would be a good time to get some furniture for his room out of your locker?"

"Now works for me. Jake's still around here, isn't he?"

At the mention of his name, Jake rounded the corner of the house with Chase in tow. "Something I can do for you ladies?"

Christy answered, "Yeah, would you follow me to my storage locker and load up some furniture for Chase? He's going to be staying here."

"Really? Miss Sally, are you going to be my foster mom?" Chase's eyes gleamed brightly in the afternoon sun.

"Well, that's the plan." Sally smiled up the boy who was growing into such a fine man.

For the second time that day, Chase hugged Sally. "Thank you so much!"

Christy looked at Chase sternly. "I'm still going to come and check on you every day that Sally isn't here. You'll still come to my house to do your laundry and get on the school bus. Mrs. Hill or I will still drive you to work. At least until Sally can get moved down here permanently."

"Yes, ma'am."

Christy hugged Chase and said, "I love you, kid. Don't ever forget that. You're always in my heart."

"I love you, too, Aunt Christy. I'm awful sorry that I made things so hard on you." Chase stared at his feet.

"Don't you ever apologize to me for that, young man. You're my blood, and I'm happy to do what's best for you. Sally being your mom is what's best for you now."

Christy turned to Sally. "This makes us sisters of a sort now." She wrapped Sally up in a fierce hug.

Jake and Chase followed Christy to her storage locker in Jake's truck while Sally went back into the house to work on making it a home. After working up a sweat, she removed her hoodie and draped it over the back of a chair. She noticed one side hung lower than the other. She reached into the pocket and pulled out a wad of cash.

"Clever, Christy." She smiled as she stuffed the money

into her jeans pocket.

CHAPTER 23

With a glance around the room, Sally looked back at Chase. They had set up his room with his own furniture in just a few minutes. "Do you feel like a real boy, now?" She teased him.

"I've felt like a real person since I met you, Miss Sally." He sat down on his bed with a grin. "It was nice of Aunt Christy to wash these sheets for me, but I'm a little old for Sponge Bob now. Do you think I could buy some new ones next time we're in town?"

Jake sat down next to him on the mattress. "I think we can handle that. What are you thinking? Minions?"

Chase laughed and smacked Jake in the face with a pillow. Jake reciprocated. Sally watched from the doorway, love filling her heart.

The happiness of the afternoon was shattered when both guys stopped what they were doing and turned their heads to the north. Jake tilted his face and sniffed the air. He sprang to his feet and shouted, "Fire!"

They ran outside and saw black smoke coming from the

barn. Chase rushed back inside and grabbed a fire extinguisher from the kitchen while Jake took the one from his truck, and Sally called 911.

With her call completed, she ran toward the barn and watched as Jake and Chase exhausted the fire extinguishers on the flames licking up one wall. The wall still smoldered, but the flames had been killed by their efforts.

She covered her mouth in anguish. "What could have happened?" she cried.

Jake glanced over his shoulder. "I smell gas. Someone set this fire. You called 911?"

"Yeah, but wouldn't you guys smell someone this close to the house? I thought you had super noses."

"The wind is blowing away from the house, or we would have. All I smell now is gas and smoke," Chase answered.

Sally heard sirens in the distance and a few minutes later saw flashing lights. The fire truck pulled to a stop. The firefighters quickly unrolled their water hoses, extinguishing the remaining smoldering embers before checking the building for hot spots.

"Miss Wagner, I'm Brian Smithers, the fire marshal. I will need a little time to take a few pictures and conduct an investigation. Do you store any flammable items in the barn?" The proper looking man in a crisp white shirt with salt and pepper hair held a pen poised above a small spiral notepad.

"I don't store anything in the barn. I haven't even been inside since I bought the property. I honestly don't know what is in there." Sally paced with her arms crossed in front of her.

"I see. Why don't you go on back up to the house, and I'll join you there after I complete my investigation. I called the sheriff, and he's on his way. Should be here shortly."

She nodded. "Thank you, Marshal. Would you like

some coffee or something? I'm going to put on a pot."

Marshal Smithers regarded her for a moment and then nodded. "That would be nice. I'll have a cup when I come up to talk to you. Thank you."

Jake put his hand on her shoulder as she turned to go. "Chase will walk you up, but I'm going to stay here with the marshal. Okay?"

"Yeah, okay." Her shoulders slumped in defeat as she lumbered back to the house.

Chase slipped his arm around her shoulders. "I'm sorry, Miss Sally. The marshal is a real smart man. He'll figure out what happened, and then Zeke will take it from there. It'll be okay. You'll see."

"I hope so. Seems I can't win with this place. I'm just glad it was the barn and not the house."

Once back in the house, Sally started brewing a pot of coffee and sat at the weathered Formica table with her head propped in her hands. Tears streamed from her eyes, down her cheeks, and splattered on the table. She found herself surrounded by the scent of lanolin. She raised her head to sniff the air.

"Chase? Do you smell lanolin?"

She looked around, but she was alone. Chase was nowhere to be found. She climbed to her feet and looked around the house. She found him on the front porch sniffing the air furiously.

"What are you doing?"

He turned to face her. "I thought maybe I could pick up a scent or something if I concentrated. Sheriff Zeke is here. I imagine he'll be up with the fire marshal directly."

"Probably so." She looked at him hard. "Maybe it's not such a good idea for you to stay here during the week after all. Something bad could happen to you. I don't want that."

He straightened to his full height, which was impressive.

"Nothing bad happens during the week. Just on the weekends. Besides, I can handle a lot of trouble. Don't you trust me?"

"Of course, I trust you! I just don't want to put you in danger. What would have happened if someone had set the house on fire with you trapped inside?" She shuddered at her gruesome thoughts.

He rested his hands on her shoulders and held her gaze. "I will be fine. There's no need for you to worry about someone like me. I'm very tough." He hugged her. "The fact that you worry about me is the main reason you will make a great foster mom. My mom always worried about me, too."

Sally stared off toward the barn for a moment. "I worry about the people I love. That's what a good person does." Then she turned and went back into the house.

She was sitting in the kitchen with her chin propped on her fist when she heard footsteps on the porch followed by the sound of the door opening and closing.

"Sweetness, where are you?" Jake's voice carried throughout the little farm house.

"I'm in the kitchen." She rose from her seat and poured four mugs of coffee. She handed one to the fire marshal, one to Jake, set one on the table for when Zeke joined them, and sipped from the last one.

"Ma'am, I'm afraid someone intentionally set that fire." Marshal Smithers frowned at her over the rim of his coffee mug. "Do you know why someone would do that?"

Sally looked at him in disbelief for a moment before she realized that not everyone knew of her feud with her distant cousin. "My cousin doesn't want me here. He lost this place due to not paying his property taxes. I own the farm fair and square, so what he wants doesn't matter."

"Have you had any more run-ins with him?" Zeke asked as he walked into the kitchen.

"Not since the last time I spoke with you, Sheriff." She

handed him the coffee mug from the table.

Zeke jotted down some notes and mumbled something to the fire marshal before returning his attention to her. "Are you all right, Sally?"

"Sure. I wasn't in the barn when the fire was set. I was having a great time with Jake and Chase here in the house." She sank back into the chair with a sigh. "I guess that'll teach me to have fun and enjoy life."

"All right, I have everything I need. I'll be sending a drone up for aerial photos to get a bird's eye view, but according to the thermal camera there are no hot spots left." Marshal Smithers nodded to each person in turn and gulped the rest of his coffee. "I'll be in touch if I need anything else, and I'll send my report to your insurance company." He set his mug in the sink and started toward the door.

"Thanks. I appreciate it." Sally looked up at him for a moment.

"I'll walk you out, Brian." Jake clapped him on the shoulder. "I sure appreciate all of your hard work today. It means a lot to me that you came personally."

"I wouldn't let anyone else handle something like this, Jake. You know these things take special care." They walked out the door deep, in conversation.

"Would you like to join me, Sheriff?" Sally indicated the chair across the table from her. "You look like you have a lot more to say."

"You're to call me Zeke, remember?" He settled in the chair across from her and wrapped both hands around his mug as he leaned forward.

"Zeke, what's on your mind? I take it you have more questions."

"Sally, the fire worries me. Someone could have been hurt. When you had your argument with Danny, what exactly did he say?"

"He told me that I was going to die here. Then he told

me there was a reason my branch of the family was written out of the will. I don't remember his exact words." She shook her head. "If he was trying to kill me, why would he have set the barn on fire instead of the house or my car?"

"Someone was giving you a warning, but I'm not convinced it was Danny. There were no traces of anything left at the scene. I need to ask you a question, and think carefully before you answer."

She quirked a brow. "Okay, you have my full attention. What's your question?"

"Did you ever hear anyone in your family talk about organized crime?"

Sally snorted. "As in the mob? No. I've never heard of anyone in my family being associated with the mob."

Zeke narrowed his eyes at her. "It was a serious question, or I wouldn't have asked it. And it could just as easily be a cartel as the mob."

"Why in the world would you think we're involved with organized crime?" Her mouth hung open. She couldn't help it.

"It's just a hunch. Would you try to get hold of your dad for me, please? I'd really like to talk to him."

"Mom and Dad are somewhere on the African continent building schools and cleaning water. I have no way of reaching them other than to mail a letter, and they only check their mailbox every few months." She shrugged. "I'm sorry."

Zeke withdrew a business card from his shirt pocket. "Please have him call me if you hear from him or get a number where I can reach him." He handed her the card. "Surely your parents will be in touch for Thanksgiving or Christmas."

"Maybe. I don't hear from them every Christmas, but they manage to call most years."

Zeke's lips tilted downward. "When was the last time you heard from your parents?"

Sally thought for a moment before answering. "I'm pretty sure the last time I talked to them was on my fortieth birthday." She thought for a moment longer. "Yeah, and I'm forty-three now, so it's been around three years."

Zeke's brows shot up to his hairline. "Three years!" He shook his head.

"We're not that close. I was much closer to Grandma and Grandpa than I ever was to Mom and Dad." She shook her head. "Not every family is close-knit."

"Well, that's not how we're going to be," Jake rumbled from behind her. He put his hands on her shoulders and kneaded her tight muscles. "Our family will be very close. We certainly won't go three years without talking to our children."

Alarm zinged through her. "Children? You said nothing about children. Jake, I'm not even sure I can have children." Sally broke away from his touch and stood to face him. "I hope this isn't a deal breaker for you."

Zeke rose from his chair. "It sounds like the two of you have a great deal to discuss. Sally, if you hear from your parents, it's important that I speak with them. In the meantime, I have paperwork to do back at the office. You know how to reach me if you need my help with anything."

"Thank you, Zeke." She took a step toward him. "I'll see you out. I could use some air."

Zeke cast an enigmatic look at Jake and then walked out the door with Sally. He turned to her when they were a few feet from his car. "Don't be too quick to jump to conclusions with Jake. He may have something entirely different in mind than the way it sounds."

"The only time we've talked about kids at all was when we were talking about me becoming Chase's foster mom. We never talked about having our own. He never mentioned wanting them before."

Zeke's lips tilted up with the hint of a smile. "Just please hear him out and don't make any rash declarations. I've been married for over thirty years, and it's difficult to repair the damage your words cause once they fly through the air and hit your mate." With that, he got into his car and drove away.

Sally watched him drive down the lane before she realized what he'd said.

Wait. Did he say mate?

CHAPTER 24

Sally ambled back in to the kitchen where she found Jake and Chase sitting at the table. They watched her enter the room with apprehension in their eyes. She looked at each of them in turn.

"Is Sheriff Zeke the alpha?"

They were both quiet for a moment before responding. "Yeah, that's what makes him such a good sheriff. He can smell it when someone lies to him. It's too bad he wasn't the sheriff when my mom went missing," Chase whispered.

Jake was more serious than she'd ever seen him. "Sally, it is of the utmost importance that he never discover you know about him. If he wants you to know, he will tell you. If he finds out you figured it out, he won't be pleasant about it."

"Asking our sheriff about his dual nature isn't high on my list of things to do these days. So, don't worry. I won't say anything to him."

"Good. It'll be better for all of us that way. Did he say anything interesting during your visit?" Jake cocked his head to the left with the expression of a little puppy.

"He thinks this fire was related to a cartel or the mob somehow. Why do you suppose he thinks such a thing?" She stood with her feet set and her hands on her hips. "Did you two smell something cartel or mob-like?"

"I'm not sure the mob has its own smell." Jake shrugged. "I don't know why he thinks it's organized crime-related, but he's hardly ever wrong. I imagine he's been digging into your family's past, and that's why he asked. His nose is no better than ours."

"It wouldn't surprise me if Danny is involved with some sort of crime syndicate. He's an evil little worm, so I imagine he would fit right in." Chase's lip curled into a frightening snarl.

"I'm sure he'll tell us when he has something concrete." Jake's shoulders bunched in irritation. "I wish he'd share what he thinks."

"He told me he needs to speak with my dad. I haven't even talked to him in at least three years, but I promised to pass along the message if and when I do hear from my parents."

Jake spun to look at her. "I still don't understand why you haven't talked to your parents in that long."

"They're unreachable when they're on a humanitarian trip. They'll call me eventually. It probably won't be any time soon."

"Well, if Zeke says he needs to talk to George, then it's important."

"Okay, if they call, I will make sure Dad talks to Zeke. Now there's something else that we need to discuss. Chase, would you please excuse us?"

He looked from one to the other and bounded to his feet. "Yes, ma'am. I'll be in my room if you need me."

Jake watched him close the door before asking, "What do we need to discuss?"

"Kids. You mentioned our kids earlier. You need to

understand that I may never be able to have babies." Tears filled her eyes. "I want them so bad. I tried with my ex-husband, but it never happened."

Jake slid his arms around her in a warm embrace. "Our kids don't need to come from your body to be ours. You've mentioned adopting Chase. Do you think he's the only child out there who needs a loving home? Someone to rely on? I just had it in my head that we would adopt a handful of kids and raise them as our own. Am I wrong in that?"

Sally sniffled. "I want kids, Jake. I've always wanted kids."

"Then it will be all right. Who knows? Once I turn you, you may conceive anyway."

"Wait. What? What do you mean by 'turn me'?"

"I mean when the time is right, I will bite you, and you'll become a werewolf like Chase and me."

Sally broke the embrace to stare at him with her mouth agape. "Let me get this straight. You plan to bite me and turn me into a furry canine." She took a step back. "Then maybe I can have puppies. Is that what you're saying?"

"Yes . . . no. I don't know. You're confusing me. Why are you so upset? Don't you want to be like us? By me turning you, you'll have our lifespan, which is a lot longer than a human's. You won't be able to catch any of the viruses that plague humans. No more colds, flu, chicken pox, none of that. You will be hearty and hale. It's entirely possible that the change will restore your uterus to perfect working order. I'm assuming that things haven't completely stopped yet, right?"

Sally stared at him. She tilted her head to the side, looked at him some more as if he were a puzzle she couldn't solve, then turned on her heal and walked out the kitchen and through the front door. It banged shut so hard the glass in the window by the door rattled.

She had almost made it to the barn when Jake caught her. He grabbed her arm and spun her around to face him.

"Where are you going? Are you crazy? What if our firebug comes back and finds you right where he wants you?"

"I guess you'll have to rescue me, my big strong man. I'm just a little ol' woman who can't make her own decisions and just follows the men folk blindly. I can't possibly have a brain and opinions of my own if I have boobs and a uterus, can I?" She wrenched her arm loose and stomped toward the barn.

"Sally, please. Talk to me. I'm lost here. What did I say to upset you?"

She whirled on him. "You're so smug. You decide I'm your mate, and then you set about making plans for our future. You've never once asked me about them. You decided you were moving in here with me, so you've been adding little things that you want. You decided we would be adopting kids, and you never once thought to include me in these plans. You even decided to have Chase move in with me. Telling me about it was an afterthought."

Jake crossed his arms over his powerful chest. "Are you seriously telling me you don't want Chase here? Because if that's what you're saying, I know for a fact that you're lying."

"Of course, I want Chase here! I love that kid! That's not my point at all. Oh!" She turned away again.

"Sally, we can fight inside just as well as outside. I don't like you being so close to a crime scene. Please come inside with me. I'll make some hot apple cider for you, and we'll talk about everything. Sound good?"

"I'll go back inside, but I can't deal with you right now."

"What are you saying?" His muscles tensed.

"I'm too angry to talk to you right now, Jake. I think you should sleep at your grandma's house tonight."

Pain flashed in his eyes at her rejection. "If that's what you really want, that's what I'll do. You know where to find me when you figure it all out."

"Thank you. I appreciate that." She sniffed, holding her

tears back with a valiant effort as she watched him climb into his truck.

"Please get in the house and lock the door. I'll talk to you in the morning. Okay?"

Her heart ached so much she thought it might stop beating. "I'll lock the door. Goodnight, Jake."

Once inside, she called out to Chase.

"You need me?" He was tense as if he already knew something was amiss. "What's up?"

"Jake is staying with his grandma tonight, so it's just you and me. I wanted to let you know."

The youth studied her for moment. "If that's what you want, then that's for the best."

He hugged her, and she couldn't hold her tears back anymore. She sobbed into Chase's shirt while the young held her.

"It'll be okay, Miss Sally. You'll see. You probably just need a good night's sleep. I bet you wake up tomorrow to things looking much better."

"I sure hope so, kid. My heart is breaking."

"Do you want to talk about it?" he asked.

"No. You deal with enough stress of your own. You don't need to borrow any of mine." She wiped her eyes. "You're right. We all need a good night's sleep. So, you go on to bed, and I'll double check all the locks."

CHAPTER 25

The next morning, Jake arrived early with three cups from a local coffee shop cradled in a drink carrier. Sally met him the door.

"I come bearing caffeine. Coffee for us and hot chocolate for Chase." He held them out to her. "Peace?"

She took a deep breath and released it with a whoosh. "All right. Come on it, and we'll talk. Thanks for the coffee."

They handed Chase his drink as he was working on patching holes in the living room and walked into the kitchen where they sat down at the table.

Jake stared at his cup for a moment before speaking. "I don't understand why you're upset, but I'm sorry."

Sally shook her head. "Do I really need to spell everything out for you? Okay, listen carefully because I will not be repeating myself. I want you to stop making plans for me without consulting me first. I don't want to find out about my own life from other people. There are so many instances where you just decide something regarding my house or my life, and I won't stand for it. I'm not wired that way."

He engulfed her small cold hand in his. "Okay. So, what would you like to discuss first?"

"How about the turning? You never mentioned it before."

"I'm sorry I haven't discussed it with you. I shouldn't have assumed you'd want to be like me. Would you rather remain human? If that's what you really want, I'll respect your wishes."

"I'll consider being turned, but it's a decision you will not make for me." She clenched her fist and shook it.

"Done. We will discuss it at length and be in full agreement before I pierce that beautiful creamy skin of yours with my manly canines. What's next?"

"Children. Why do you think it may be possible for me to have kids if you turn me? My doctor told me that my uterus is tipped and the chances of me ever getting pregnant are slim to none. Why would turning me change that?"

"Werewolves have longer life spans and heal much quicker than humans. It seems logical to me that turning you would fix whatever woman stuff you have that needs healed or corrected."

"So, let's say that's the way it works. Would I have babies or puppies?"

He stared at her for a moment. "Is that a real question?"

She blinked at him. "Yes. Why would I ask you a fake question?"

"Werewolves have babies just like humans do. The dual nature doesn't come into being until puberty. So, for all intents and purposes, the kid is human for the first ten or twelve years of life."

She nodded thoughtfully.

"Next issue?"

"Do you actually love me or just the idea of loving me? We didn't see each other for a really long time. I'm worried that maybe you built me up in your mind into some amazing woman that I'm not." Sally examined her coffee cup to keep from looking at him.

"Sweetness, you should know better." He gently turned her face toward him with a single finger on her chin. "I love you, not the idea of you. I've always loved you. I was working up the courage to kiss you when your grandparents died, and I didn't get to see you again for a few decades. Kind of ruined my plans."

Her eyes widened. "You were planning to give me my first kiss?" She clasped her hands together and brought them to her heart. "I wish your plans had been realized. My first kiss would have been so much more special if it had come from you."

"Well, I can't change the past. But I can make sure I'm the only one who kisses you from now on. If that's what you want." He grinned sheepishly.

"Yeah, that's what I want." She leaned over the table and kissed him in a sweet little caress.

"If you doubt my love for you, then I'm doing something wrong." He kissed her deeply. "A woman should never question her mate's love and devotion. I love you mind, body, and soul. Let me show you how much I love every single inch of you."

She allowed him a deep kiss before she pushed him away. "That sounds great, but I need to process all of this. I've been independent for a long time. I control my own life. I'm having trouble with you swooping in and making decisions. So, I would rather not get physical right now."

He stared at her for a moment, his mouth agape.

"I'm going to go paint the kitchen today. Would you like to help?" she asked.

He wrinkled his brow and looked like he was thinking for a moment before he answered. "I'd be happy to help you paint today."

By dinnertime, the kitchen was a sunny yellow, and she

was stretching out the rooster border to be sure she'd bought enough.

CHAPTER 26

Sally was dreaming of snuggling with her wolf on a bed of rose petals when an obnoxious banging sound awakened her. She opened her eyes and peered at the alarm clock. 6:30 a.m. She rolled over to complain to Jake and found his side of the bed empty.

She crawled out of bed, put on Jake's shirt, and wandered out into the living room to see what was transpiring.

"Good morning, Sally," Zeke said as he handed her a cup of coffee. "You need to get dressed. The ATF will be here in a few minutes."

She stood dumbfounded for a moment. "ATF?"

"The Bureau of Alcohol, Tobacco, Firearms, and Explosives. Sally, go put some clothes on. Your own clothes. Hurry up. You don't have much time. Go!" Zeke's fierce gaze left no room for argument.

She sprinted to her bedroom and dressed in her dirty jeans and an oversized sweatshirt. She was slipping her feet into her shoes when she heard another firm knock at her front door. She took a deep breath and went to see the ATF agents who had just entered her home.

"Miss Wagner?" At her nod, the tall middle-aged blonde man said, "I'm Agent Steel, and this is Agent Ford. We have a warrant to search your barn."

"A search warrant? Why?" She clutched the paper Agent Steel had given her with shaking hands.

Agent Ford pulled some photos from her briefcase and handed them to Sally. "These are aerial photos that were taken by the fire department after your fire yesterday. Do you see anything unusual in them?"

Sally examined the photos. "I see the barn has a big hole in the roof and there are some wooden crates inside. Then I see a faint path through the south pasture between the woods and barn."

Agent Steel watched her closely. "What do you think made the path?"

"It's weird. Kind of big for an animal trail. Maybe we have hikers? Who would want to hike to the barn and back?" She shared a look with Zeke. "Why don't you tell me what's going on, and I'll try to help however I can."

Agent Ford shook her head. "It doesn't work that way. We need for you to tell us how you use the barn."

"I don't use the barn. It doesn't look safe. I've been concentrating on repairing the house so I can move into it this coming spring. I plan to tear the barn down once the house is done."

"Sheriff, we'd appreciate it if you'd stay with Miss Wagner while we search the barn." Agent Steel placed a hard hat with an attached light on his head.

"Wait! I want to go, too! Don't I have the right to be present while my property is being searched?"

Agent Ford shook her head. "You may wait outside the barn while we search it if you like, but you may not enter."

Sally met the brunette's gaze. "Fine. I'll wait for you outside the barn. I want to know what's going on just as much as you."

They made their way to the barn as the sun was peaking over the horizon. The agents entered the structure, and Sally could hear what sounded like wooden crates being pried open. The search took less than fifteen minutes.

Agent Steel emerged from the barn with his lips pressed together in a tight line. Agent Ford followed carrying a rectangular metal box that looked like some sort of weapon.

"Do you recognize this item, Miss Wagner?" Agent Ford asked.

"No. What is it? Some sort of rocket launcher?" Sally clasped her hands together to stop their shaking.

"This is a M320 grenade launcher with the serial number removed, Miss Wagner. It's illegal to distribute or own. You have several cases of them in your barn."

Sally felt the color drain from her face and sweat dampen her skin. "Agents, I have never seen anything like that in my life. Please believe that I don't know anything about such things."

Zeke stepped forward and addressed the agents. "Perhaps it would be best to continue this conversation up at the house."

"Yes. We could go into the kitchen and talk. I'll make some coffee." Sally spoke in a quiet voice.

"That would be very nice, Miss Wagner. Thank you." Agent Ford's petite frame perked up at the mention of coffee. The woman looked like she'd been rolled out of bed in the middle of the night and thrown on the first outfit she found. Her black slacks and jacket were rumpled, and her white blouse was buttoned crooked.

They walked back to the house where Sally led them to the kitchen and started a strong pot of coffee. Once her coffee maker was huffing away, she took her place at the table.

Agent Steel regarded her silently for a moment. "What do you know about the illegal arms trade?"

Sally furrowed her brows. "Nothing. I wouldn't know where to sell one of those things if my life depended on it."

Zeke stood and filled mugs with coffee for each of them. He handed them out and began pacing. "Agents, with your permission, I'd like to try."

Agent Steel sighed. "Well, this is your territory and sometimes the end justifies the means. Go ahead and do it your way, Sheriff, but this part isn't going into the official report."

Zeke returned to the table and straddled a chair with his hands resting on the back. He held Sally's gaze as he spoke. "Those weapons are a big-time payday for someone. You have several million dollars in contraband waiting in your barn for someone to retrieve. We never would have known about it without the drone photos. The agents here are trying to figure out if you are the one selling military grade arms or if someone else has been using your barn."

Her eyes widened as she stood up. "You honestly think I'm selling those grenade things? I don't know the first thing about them." She paced the kitchen.

"We're here to get some answers, Miss Wagner." Agent Ford's voice was soft and reassuring. "We're not accusing you of any wrong doing. The sheriff is confident in your innocence in this situation. We're simply trying to find out who is storing illegal weapons on your property. You haven't owned this place long enough for the crates to have collected as much dust as they have."

"My cousin, Danny, has been very vocal about not wanting me here. He owned this place until the county took it for unpaid taxes. Have you spoken with him?"

"Do you believe the launchers are his?" Agent Steel sat forward with his pen poised over his little notebook.

"No. I think he's too lazy to put that much effort into anything. He might have let someone use the place, though.

I can see him doing that." Sally bit her lip. "He's a mean little man, but I don't know that he would get involved with illegal weapons."

"You give that little weasel too much credit," Jake said from the doorway.

"Jake, where've you been? I was worried when you were gone."

"Sorry to worry you, Sweetness. The sheriff wanted Chase and me to go help Christy round up her horses. Someone opened her stable and let all ten horses out. They were all over the place. Chase is still out there looking for the last couple."

Sally blinked up at Jake. "That's weird. Why would anyone do that?"

Zeke cursed beneath his breath. "I think it's all connected. Someone was trying to keep me busy. They didn't count on me calling the ATF in, though. It's my guess someone was trying to distract me long enough to get their munitions moved."

Agent Steel chuckled. "We have a couple men out there watching the barn. It's more than just grenade launchers. There are several cases of M420 carbines out there, too. All without serial numbers."

"M420 carbines? I'm afraid I don't follow, Agent." Sally refilled her coffee cup and topped everyone else's off, as well.

"M420 carbine rifles are fully automatic guns used by the military. Those grenade launchers can be attached to them via the Picatinny rail making them even more lethal. We just need to figure out who put them there."

Jake rested his hands on her shoulders and gently rubbed her knotted muscles.

"Who would even buy so many illegal guns?" Sally's brow furrowed as she sipped her coffee.

Agent Steel answered, "Mexican drug cartels pay big bucks for weapons like these. They are in a constant state of war against each other. My guess is your barn was a place to store the guns until they could be shipped to Mexico."

"And you think Danny did this?" Sally asked turning to Jake.

He huffed. "I don't think he is dealing them himself because that's too much work, but I do think he let someone else use the barn for a generous fee."

Agent Ford turned to Sally. "We've already looked at your bank records, and we're confident you aren't involved. You barely have enough in there to pay your mortgage. We'll have someone go over Danny's accounts, as well. Can you think of anyone else who might be involved?"

Sally thought for a moment. "You might want to check out Ray Jones. He and Chase's Aunt Christy own the adjoining land. It was their horses that got out this morning."

"Thank you, Miss Wagner. We'll check him out. We're confiscating the weapons, but we'd like your permission to put up some cameras around your property to catch whoever comes to collect their contraband in the act."

"Of course. Whatever you need to do. I want them gone. I'm worried about what will happen when the criminals come to get their guns and find them gone. Are we in danger? I have a minor child living here and need to ensure his safety." Sally's voice rose in pitch with each word she spoke.

"We will monitor the situation via the surveillance equipment and keep an agent close by."

"I hope this gets resolved soon. I'm going to be taking classes through the foster care system, and I don't want anything to ruin my chances of becoming a foster parent. And what about the fire? It doesn't make sense that whoever left the guns there would start the fire."

"No. I think whoever set the fire had no idea anything was inside. So, we're dealing with two different groups here." Agent Steel rubbed his chin as he spoke.

Zeke stood and stretched. "Well, it looks like we have a lot of work to do. Sally, I'm going to have some of my men stationed up the hill a ways to keep an eye on things and make sure you and Chase are safe. I'm assuming Jake won't leave your side."

"You got that right. Sally is my main priority. No one gets to her without going through me first." Jake slid his arm around her shoulders and pulled her to him.

Agent Ford stood and gathered all of the photos and paperwork. "We'll be in touch, Miss Wagner. Don't worry. We will get to the bottom of this."

Zeke and the agents all walked out the door leaving Sally and Jake alone.

"Well, Sweetness, it looks like your farm wasn't abandoned after all."

CHAPTER 27

Sally was just setting breakfast in front of Jake and Chase when she heard the crunch of tires on rock coming up the driveway. Jake rose and peered out the window.

"It's Ma from the diner," he said tilting his head to one side.

"Why would Ma be coming for a visit?" Sally shook her head and grabbed another plate from the cupboard, set it on the table, and joined Jake in the living room.

She opened the front door before Ma could even knock.

"Good morning, Ma. Come on in. We were just about to sit down to breakfast. Would you like to join us?" Sally asked.

Ma entered the house and then turned and secured the door. "No. Thank you kindly for the invite, though. You got yourself a heap of trouble, Bunny girl." She raked her hands through her short gray hair. "You done ticked off the wrong folks."

"But I didn't do anything, Ma. Someone set fire to the

barn and then the next thing I knew I was being questioned by federal authorities." Sally's voice rose with each word.

Jake stepped forward and asked, "Ma, what have you heard?"

She took a deep breath, held it for a few seconds, and then let it out with a whoosh. "The Martinez brothers was in the diner this mornin'. I overheard them talkin' about a lost shipment of somethin'. They said it was found on Dale's place and Bunny gave it to the feds. They real mad, Jake. Real mad. They want the money the shipment woulda made."

She turned to Sally and took her hands. "Bunny, I owe it to yer granny. We got to get you outta here. I know you ain't got the kind of cash they'll demand."

"Ma, please come into the kitchen and we'll talk about this," Sally said walking that way.

She poured Ma a cup of coffee and they all settled at the table.

"Sally is well protected here, Ma." Jake steepled his fingers and tapped his lips. "The feds have left surveillance equipment, and Zeke has men stationed on the hill. Then there's Chase and me. We're pretty tough."

"It don't matter how tough you are or who is where. Them Martinez brothers is bad news. I don't know what was lost, but they somehow found out you had it. These ain't the type of folks who politely ask you to return their stuff. The fact you had it at all is enough to get you killed."

"I'd like to know how they found out Miss Sally had that stuff," Chase said. "No one knew it was here until early this morning."

"That's a good point, Chase," Jake said pulling out his cell phone. "Someone with the fire department, the sheriff's office, or the ATF had to have told them. I'm calling Zeke."

"Wouldn't they go after whoever had their shipment last? That's the person who had to have stashed it here."

Sally stood and paced the room. "You don't suppose Danny . . ."

"No, but I bet he rented the barn out to someone, though," Jake said dialing. He turned and walked into the bedroom.

"I don't understand how you are involved in all this, Ma," Sally said.

The old woman sighed and grabbed a slice of toast from the plate on the table. She tore a small piece off and chewed it slowly before answering.

"Your grandparents were good people. Sometimes good people do bad things. Just remember that, okay?"

Jake returned, slipping the phone back in his pocket. "Zeke is on his way. It won't take him long. He's up at Christy's again."

"Why is he at Aunt Christy's?" Chase visibly paled. "Is she okay?"

"Yeah, she's fine. Ray got drunk last night and threatened to shoot the neighbor's rooster for making too much noise so early this morning." Jake grinned. "Mrs. Barret is liable to fill Ray's backside full of buckshot if he looks crossways at that rooster now."

Their chuckling was interrupted by heavy boots on the wooden porch. A firm knock sounded on the door. Jake went to let Zeke in while Ma blanched.

"I got no problem with Sheriff Zeke, but I don't like lawmen in general. They're a nosy bunch."

Jake and the sheriff entered the kitchen with their mouths set in grim lines.

"Good morning, everyone," Zeke said. "It's nice to see you again, Ma. I understand you have some information for me."

Ma looked directly into Zeke's eyes and held his steady gaze. "The Martinez brothers were in my diner this mornin' and they have a blood grudge against Sally here. I heard them say somethin' about a lost shipment that somebody found at Dale's old place. They were talkin' about how Sally gave whatever that shipment was to the feds. They think she was hidin' it here until she could sell it. She in trouble, Sheriff. We need to get her outta here!"

"Did you hear them say anything else? Like maybe where the shipment had been headed when it was lost?" Zeke tapped keys on his phone while he spoke.

"No, I didn't hear nothing 'bout that. I heard 'em say they would get either their money or blood from Bunny, and I jumped in the car and came right over. I have a safe place she can stay. Aint got runnin' water, but she'd be safe."

"She's fine for right now. I called the ATF agents, and they're sending more people to keep an eye on the place."

"Sheriff, someone had to tip the Martinez brothers off about what was found in the barn. We need to find out who." Jake came to stand behind Sally and rubbed the tight muscles in her shoulders.

"I'm betting it was someone from the fire department. They have several . . . new people on the truck. I'll look into it, though. Steel's ATF team is beyond reproach. I've known all of them for years."

Zeke took Sally's hands. "Your safety is our top priority. We have this area secured. Nothing will happen to you here."

Sally smiled at him for a moment. "You want to catch them in the act, don't you? They won't come if I'm not here, and you need to have evidence to arrest them. Am I right?"

"You are a smart cookie, Sally."

"Thank you. Here's my problem with your fire department theory. How would anyone from there know about the ATF at all? They arrived after the fire department was long gone."

Zeke scratched his chin. "Fair point, Sally. I'll talk to Steel and have him look into his people to see if any have a connection to the Martinez brothers. I'll do the same with my people at the sheriff's department."

"Sheriff, I think you should look at Uncle Ray, too." Chase said. "He has some rough looking associates who come around when Aunt Christy is at work. He always owes them money for whatever reason. He tries to be sneaky, but I have good hearing."

Ma laughed and patted his shoulder. "That you do, my boy. And keen eyes, too. Keep 'em open and watch for trouble."

"Could you identify these associates of Ray's if you saw their pictures?" Zeke asked.

"Yeah. I'm sure I could. When do you want me to look at them?"

"Why don't you come with me now? I'll bring you back once we're finished. This could be our best lead yet." Zeke nodded to Chase.

Jake cleared his throat. "Ray lives close enough that he could have been watching us from a distance, and we were so distracted we'd never have known."

Zeke nodded. "True enough. Damn, I hate it when things get overly complicated."

Chase stood. "I'm ready to go whenever you are, Sheriff."

"Right then. Let's get this figured out, so we can enjoy the holiday in a few days." They headed for the front door. "I'll see you all soon. And Ma, please call me if you hear anything else that's interesting."

Ma's shoulders slumped. "I will, Sheriff. It's not fair that Bunny got caught in the middle like this. I sure do wish she'd come with me and let me hide her."

Jake nodded to Sally. "I'll walk these guys out. Then I'll patrol the perimeter and make sure everything is as it should be. I have my key, so you can go ahead and lock the door." The three men walked out the door leaving the two women deep in discussion.

Sally rested her hand on Ma's. "Thank you for the offer, Ma. I really appreciate you worrying about me like that. The sheriff is right, though. Those thugs won't come here if they think I'm gone. Something tells me they would know I'm not here and track me down to wherever you plan to take me."

"But . . ." Ma stammered.

"Thank you, Ma. I need to stay here and face whatever is coming at me head-on. I'm tired of fighting just for the right to have a peaceful place to live. This is my farm, and I will not be chased off!" Sally stomped her foot.

Ma smiled and hugged her. "You are Fern's granddaughter. No doubt about it. Take this." She slipped a compact semi-automatic Smith & Wesson nine-millimeter pistol into Sally's hand. "You may need it, Bunny."

Sally gave her a small smile and nodded. "This, I will gratefully accept. Fully loaded, I assume?"

"It's got twelve in the magazine and one in the chamber, Bunny. Be sure to hit what you aim at. Yer granny taught you to shoot, right?"

"Yes. She taught me many things that I'm really coming to appreciate." Sally dropped the magazine, checked the load, and slammed it home again with a flourish. "Perfect. Now you better go. You don't want to be here when those Martinez boys show up."

"Yer right. I'm out. Take care, Bunny." Ma hugged her one last time and hurried out the door.

Sally slipped the pistol into her jeans pocket and slid the deadbolt on the door into place.

CHAPTER 28

Sally walked around the house making certain all of the windows were secure. The pistol in her pocket made her feel a small measure of safety. She put their uneaten breakfast in the refrigerator and cleaned the kitchen.

Looking around the house with an eye for defense, she propped a broom inside her bedroom door, hung her large cast iron skillet on a nail just inside the kitchen door, and moved her rifle to rest behind the front door. She stood back and examined her weapons placement with skepticism. She dug through the pile of packing material and found some Styrofoam, which she placed beneath each window. An intruder wouldn't make it past the white fluffy stuff without making some noise.

Sally turned as she heard a key slide into the lock on the front door. Jake let himself in a moment later. After he slid the deadbolt into place, she gestured to her security measures and asked, "What do you think? It's not ADT, but it's better than nothing."

Jake took her in his arms and held her to his chest. "I'm not going to let anyone get you, Sweetness. You are safe with me. Now and forever."

"I just thought I should be proactive. We have to sleep sometime." Sally rested her head on his powerful chest and listened to the soothing rhythm of his heart.

He kissed the top of her head and whispered, "I love you, Sally Sue. We are going to enjoy a long happy life together. I'm not going to let a couple two-bit gun runners keep us from the future we deserve."

They both jumped when a firm knock on the door interrupted their quiet moment. They turned to peer out the window and found Zeke and Chase staring back at them. Jake opened the door and stood aside so they could enter.

"Well, did you find anything useful?"

The sheriff clapped Chase on the back. "He identified two of Ray's associates. Vincent and Micah Martinez. We found our connection."

Jake nodded stroking his chin. "That connection explains how they found out about the seizure assuming Ray has been spying on us. He doesn't strike me as the spying type, but he certainly isn't honorable."

Chase clenched his fists. "He's a worm and a bully. Aunt Christy deserves so much better than him. It makes sense that he was causing distractions every time something happened here. He knows the neighbor calls the sheriff every time a horse gets out."

Zeke nodded. "If he's into these guys for a load of money, he may have figured he could have Sally settle his debt for him by turning her over to them. They have a rap sheet a mile long. These guys are bad news."

"Is that enough to get a warrant to search Ray's house, Sheriff?" Sally asked.

"No, but it's enough to make him a person of interest," Zeke replied. "That means I can go have a talk with him and see if he cracks under pressure."

"I hope he breaks like an egg!" Chase stomped into his bedroom and slammed the door.

Sally rolled her eyes. "Someone is finally letting today's stress get to him."

Zeke laughed. "Yeah. He's a good boy, but he's still a teen. That kind of behavior is commonplace with kids that age."

Jake squared his shoulders. "What's our next step? We need to get this resolved, so Sally can feel safe in her home."

"I've doubled the surveillance here. I spoke with Steel, and he concurs that Ray is probably the missing piece to our puzzle. The question is how did he know so much unless he was here watching?"

Jake's face brightened. "I have an idea of how he may have known. We need to search for trail cameras and tree stands. He could watch us from a distance with those things."

Zeke cocked his head. "You're right. We've searched this place, but I don't know if anyone has looked in the trees. That's a great idea, Jake."

"Well, I did learn a few things when I was in Air Force Operations Intelligence."

Sally's eyes widened and her mouth dropped open in shock. "I didn't know you were in the Air Force! I certainly didn't know you worked in the intelligence field. There's so much we need to learn about each other. I feel like we've barely scratched the surface."

"Sweetness, we will learn everything about each other before you know it. The most important thing you need to know about me is that I love you. The second most important thing you need to know is that I can and will protect you."

Zeke patted her shoulder. "Jake is a capable man. I'm glad he's always on my side. He can be lethal if he needs to. That's a good thing, Sally."

"Yes, it is. I'm just surprised. That's all. I look forward to settling in here and getting to know all of you better. I missed this place and all of the people who give it character."

"We welcome you home, Sally." Zeke said. "Now, I'm going to go talk to Ray and have my people start searching the trees. I'll be in touch."

Zeke opened the door and took a step out. Before he closed it behind him, he turned back to Sally. "Don't you fret. We'll get this figured out. In the meantime, don't do anything rash like wandering around by yourself." He closed the door and sauntered off to his patrol car.

Jake took Sally's hands in his large warm ones and peered into her eyes. "We will get through this. Then you, me, and Chase will make a happy little family. We'll have a good life here on the farm. In the meantime, I'm here for you, and I'm not going anywhere."

"I appreciate that. I want you to know that I am not helpless, though. I feel like the princess that you guys are trying to lock in the tower. I won't live like that. It's not in me to sit back and rely on others to solve my problems. I will fight beside you, but I refuse to hide behind you."

Jake laughed. "I don't doubt that for a minute, Sweetness. That fierce streak of yours is one of the things I find irresistible about you." He put his hands on her hips and smiled. "I take it you know how to use this pistol I feel in your pocket?"

"Yes. I know how, and I won't hesitate."

"That's my girl. I don't know where you got it, and I don't care. I'm just glad you have it."

Sally's lips tipped up as she replied, "Thanks, Jake. I feel better having something with me. Like I said, I will fight."

"Well, the fight hasn't come to us yet, so let's get the living room painted. We might even have time to paint the rest of the rooms if all stays quiet today."

"That sounds great. I'll go get Chase and see if he wants to help. The physical labor might take his mind off Ray."

Jake hugged her. "That kind of logic is what will make you a great mom. Chase is lucky to have you."

At the end of the day, Sally surveyed their progress with satisfaction. They had painted the living room sky blue and the bedrooms soothing sage green. They painted the bathroom the original pink color in honor of her grandma who had loved that color so much. Then they hung the rooster border in the kitchen. The place was finally starting to look like home.

Jake came up behind her and slipped his arms around her waist. "I think it looks good. Do you like it?"

Sally relaxed her tired body into his immense strength. "I love it! I still can't believe you had these amazing colors just lying around your shop."

"I do a lot of remodels, and some folks want every room painted a different color. I can't return half a bucket of paint, so I squirrel it away. I'm certainly not going to waste good paint." He leaned down and kissed the shell of her ear. "I think the blue was the right choice for the living room. It's cheerful without being in your face. Pretty much any kind of furniture will go with it."

Sally smiled as Chase came into the room. "I'm all done with my room, Miss Sally. It looks good. I didn't think I'd like green, but I have to say it's kinda nice."

"I'm glad you like it. Sage green always makes me feel relaxed. I read an article once that said green was one of the most soothing colors because it makes us think of nature."

Chase grinned. "Maybe that's why I like it. It feels like home."

"Home. I like the sound of that. I always want you to feel at home here, Chase." Sally's eyes burned with unshed tears. "We all need a place to feel safe and call home. You're always welcome here."

"Oh, Miss Sally, you're too much." He leaned in and

kissed her cheek before wandering back into the kitchen.

She heard the rumble of Jakes laugh through his chest. "Yes, Sweetness, you are too much. I'm so glad you stayed true to yourself."

She tilted her head and sniffed the air before asking, "Jake, do you smell apple pie?"

"Yeah, your grandma must be happy with the way things turned out, too."

CHAPTER 29

Thanksgiving at Mrs. Hill's house became a festive affair. She had the dining room decorated with paper turkeys and plastic pilgrims. The table was decked out with a delicate lace tablecloth and place settings of her finest stoneware. Crystal glasses and serving bowls gleamed in the light. Food covered every available surface. Sally had a difficult time finding space for her apple and peanut butter pies.

Most of their friends and neighbors were there. Everyone gathered around the table. Sally and Jake found themselves sitting across from Zeke and Martha. Once grace was said, dishes were passed, and plates filled, Mrs. Hill stood and demanded attention.

"Thank you all for coming. I would like to take this opportunity to share with you some of the things for which I'm thankful. I'm so thankful that Sally Sue decided to attend a tax auction where she bought her grandparents' farm. Since her arrival, my grandson has stayed busy and happy. I always thought the two of them belonged together.

Now, they agree with me."

She smiled and held up her glass of sparkling cider. "Thank you for coming home, Sally Sue. You've already touched so many lives. I have a feeling you'll touch many more before you are settled in. Welcome home."

Everyone else's voices echoed "welcome home" as Sally's face blazed in embarrassment.

Jake leaned over during the meal and whispered, "You sure have made Grandma happy. If I wasn't completely in love with you before, I would be now."

After stuffing themselves silly, Sally and Jake joined Zeke on Mrs. Hill's back deck.

Zeke sighed and patted his belly. "That was a fine meal. I ate more today than I've eaten all week. Sally, your peanut butter pie is amazing."

Sally blushed. "Thanks. I can give you the recipe if you like."

"Better give it to Martha. She's the baker. It wouldn't even look like a pie if I tried to make it." Zeke peered through the sliding glass door. "I see she's busy bending young Chase's ear about something right now. He might be grateful if you interrupted them."

Jake cleared his throat. "Before you do that, we should talk to Zeke about our situation." He turned to the sheriff. "We have make-shift security measures, but I'm worried. How sophisticated are these Martinez brothers you mentioned? Have you heard anything else?"

Zeke scratched his chin as he thought. "They have been in and out of jail, but I haven't dealt with them much, myself. Most of their crimes are committed in the city limits of River Falls, and their police force deals with them. Very few charges have stuck. Their old man keeps a good lawyer on retainer."

"Do they work with anyone else? I'm just trying to wrap my mind around what to expect," Sally said.

"They have before, but it's usually just the two of them.

From what I understand, not many people can stand to be around them. They're not pleasant guys."

Jake nodded. "Thanks for the information and all of your hard work. I'll be glad when this is all over and we can concentrate on the simple things in life."

Sally giggled. "You mean like home rehabilitation?"

An answering grin lifted Jake's lips. "Yeah. Like home rehabilitation."

Zeke chuckled and clapped both of them on the shoulders. "We'll get to the bottom of everything, and then you can concentrate on fun things like shingles and light fixtures."

Sally hugged the sheriff. "Thanks for everything, Zeke. I will get that recipe to Martha in a few days. Right now, I need to go home and take a nap."

He nodded. "Have a good evening, you two."

"Happy Thanksgiving, Zeke," Sally replied.

After they said their goodbyes to everyone, they waddled to Jake's truck and drove back to the farmhouse.

Putting away several containers bulging with leftovers from Mrs. Hill's house, Sally smiled. She felt like she was part of a family again. It had been a long time since she had been so happy. Excited about the future, she joined Jake and Chase in the living room to look at paint colors.

CHAPTER 30

They were finishing their supper when both men went still. They turned in unison toward Chase's bedroom. Jake held a finger to his lips and nodded to the boy. They didn't make a single sound rising from their chairs. Chase inclined his head toward Sally. At Jake's nod, he took a position along the wall just outside his bedroom door.

Sally pulled her pistol from her pocket and rested it on her leg so it wasn't obvious. She remained quiet as Jake entered the bedroom. She heard a grunt followed by a thump, the squeak of Styrofoam, and then a groan. Soon after, Jake dragged Danny into the kitchen.

"Look who I found breaking into the house." Jake tossed him to the kitchen floor.

"What the hell are you doing here, Danny?" Sally demanded. "I have enough trouble without you adding to it!"

Danny climbed to his feet and glared at her. "You don't belong here! You've ruined everything! I told you to leave, but no. You had to be stubborn. Now you've got goons on the hunt for you, and if they don't get you, they're coming for me next. You should have stayed away!"

At that moment Sally finally noticed the crazed look in his eyes. Danny reached into his jacket pocket and withdrew a bottle full of kerosene with a rag stuffed in the top. He took a lighter from his front pocket before she could say anything. She watched in horror as he flicked the lighter. Then there was a blur as Danny was knocked to the floor and the bottle and lighter wrenched from his grasp.

Sally was shocked at how quickly Chase and Jake had moved. Jake had Danny pinned to the floor by his throat while Chase was holding the bottle and lighter.

"What the hell are the two of you doing here, anyway? You don't belong here!" Danny screeched.

"We're looking out for Miss Sally, you piece of trash," Chase snarled.

Danny smiled evilly. "Have you heard from your mommy lately, Chase?"

The question put Sally over the edge. With a snarl she clicked off the safety and pointed her gun at her cousin. "Why would you ask such a question, Danny? Do you know something about Chase's mom?"

"Get away from me, you crazy bitch!" Danny yelped.

"Not until you answer my question! I swear to God that I will shoot your favorite parts right off of you! Now answer my question! Do you know something about Chase's mom?" Sally screamed at him.

"She died," Danny whined.

"When did she die, Danny?" Jake snarled.

"It was that night that everyone thought she left. She called and said she needed to talk to me privately, so I went to pick her up so we could go have a private conversation. She fell, hit her head, and died. I didn't know what else to do, so I brought her here and buried her," Danny sniveled.

Chase regained his ability to speak and knocked both

Jake and Sally out of the way. "Where is she buried?" Chase demanded.

"In the low spot behind the barn where nothing ever grows," Danny finally choked out.

"So, all of these years, you knew she didn't leave me. You knew she died. And yet you still tormented me every time you saw me. You convinced most of the folks around here that my own mother didn't even want me, so I must be no good," Chase seethed.

"When she called and asked me to take her someplace private to talk, I knew I had to take her to the cave. It's the most private place in the world. I was hoping we'd get it on again, but that's not what she had in mind."

"What did she want to tell you?" Sally's voice was reasonably steady for the number of emotions crashing through her.

"Pam wanted to tell me that I had a son. She thought it was the right thing to do." Danny shook his head and spat.

"What?" Sally moved the gun closer. "Did you just say that you're Chase's father? How can that possibly be true?"

Danny's smile was vile. "We made him the usual way. Pam and Tony had split up. I convinced her to go out with me. We drank a little moonshine and had hot sweaty sex in the cave by the creek. I knocked her up, but she thought the kid was Tony's. She went back to him so he could raise his child." Danny laughed, a sound that held no humor.

Chase shook his head. "No, that can't be true. You're a horrible person! You can't possibly be my father!"

"Yeah, well finding out you were mine didn't make my day either, kid," Danny snarled.

"We're getting off topic, and this is important," Sally interrupted. "So, Danny, you were talking about why Pam called. Please continue."

"That's why she called me the night she died. Tony had a doctor's appointment that day and found out he couldn't have kids, so the brat there couldn't possibly be his. He beat the crap out of her and then took their car to rob a liquor store."

"What did you do when she told you?" Jake's face was red and his body vibrated with leashed violence.

Danny curled his lip. "I told her she couldn't have any money. There was no way I was paying child support. I'm not cut out to be a dad, but I would gladly give her another pleasure ride any time she wanted."

Chase's face turned purple. "How exactly did my mother die?"

"I told you. She fell and hit her head."

"HOW?"

Danny snorted. "So, you want the gory details? Okay. She told me you were my kid. I told her she couldn't have any money. She got real mad and yelled at me. She called me all kinds of names. Said she didn't call me for money. Just thought I might like to know I had a kid. Then she took a swing at me with her purse. I ducked. She slipped and fell. She hit her head on a rock. She was dead when I checked for a pulse." Danny's face showed no remorse at all.

Jake's face was a mask of fury as he said, "Sally, get some rope. We're taking Danny to the barn."

"What? You can't be serious! You aren't planning to kill me, are you?"

"You came here with every intention of burning down the house and hurting Sally. I'm not entirely convinced that you didn't kill Pam in the first place. Why else wouldn't you just take her to the hospital and let the coroner take care of her?"

They were still puzzling it out when Danny slid across the room. A sudden wind blew through the house and slammed Danny up against the wall. It whirled him around and slammed him hard against the floor. Then he was drawn up and hung limply against the wall by some unseen force.

He stared straight in front of him and screamed, "I'm sorry! I'm sorry! I killed her! She said she didn't want to be with me, and I killed her! Oh God, please don't hurt me!"

"Who are you talking to, Danny?" Sally asked.

"Why? Don't you see him?" Danny yelped. "It's your grandpa, and he's hopping mad!"

"Since Grandpa has been dead for thirty years, I think he can do whatever he feels best with you," Sally answered, feeling much calmer than she probably should. The smell of lanolin permeated the house.

"Please Sally, make him stop!"

She sighed. "Grandpa, please put Danny down. If you kill him, we will have a lot of explaining to do. I refuse to bury him behind the barn. I don't want him anywhere near this place."

Danny fell in a heap to the floor. He looked up at Sally with haunted eyes. "Follow me. I'll show you where I buried Pam."

CHAPTER 31

Sally put her pistol back in her pocket, grabbed some flashlights from her newly organized junk drawer, and they all filed outside. On the way to the barn Sally asked, "So is this why you didn't want anyone else here? You were afraid of Pam being discovered? Or was it the guns hidden in the barn?"

Danny grunted, but didn't really answer. Sally didn't trust the calculating gleam in his eyes. As they rounded the side of the barn to the back lot, he pulled a knife out of his boot, grabbed her by the hair, and pressed the blade to her throat.

"Don't even think about pulling that gun of yours on me again. I'll have your throat slit by the time your hand reaches your pocket," Danny snarled in her ear.

Both Chase and Jake stopped moving. Sally could hear growls coming from deep in their throats. "That is the final nail in your coffin, Danny," Jake said.

Danny's hand trembled violently and the blade nicked Sally's throat. His hand froze when Chase morphed into his wolf form, shredding his clothes as his body changed. The wolf leapt on him, and they all tumbled to the ground. Jake took Sally's arm and dragged her away as Chase mauled the man who murdered his mother.

Sally quickly recovered. "Chase, you have to stop this! Do not kill that little weasel. You don't want his death on your conscience! He deserves to rot in prison! Please stop!"

Chase looked at Sally and finally disengaged from Danny. The slimy worm was bleeding from several places and unconscious, but still breathing.

"I'm going to call the sheriff. I suggest you get back up to the house and put some clothes on before I have to explain why I have one naked man and another one unconscious in my barnyard," Sally said.

"Yeah, that's a good idea." Breathing hard, Chase stopped in front of Sally and took her hand. "Miss Sally, I would've killed him if it hadn't been for you. I want you to know that."

"I don't doubt you, Chase. That's why I had to stop you. You don't need to live with that kind of guilt for the rest of your life. You deserve better than that."

He nodded and took off in a run back to the house.

Sally pulled her phone out of her pocket and dialed. She reported that her cousin had tried to hurt her, burn down her house, and had been injured in the process. She also told the dispatcher that he had confessed to a murder. She hung up after being assured that the sheriff would be there soon.

"Where are the people who are supposed to be guarding this place? We should have seen someone by now." Sally looked around her with worry.

"I wondered about that, too. We'll ask Zeke when he gets here."

Feeling exhausted, Sally turned to Jake and wrapped her arms around his waist. "Tonight was certainly eventful. I learned my cousin is a murderer, and a woman is buried in my barnyard. If that wasn't enough, Grandpa's ghost beat the crap out of my murdering cousin who buried the woman behind my barn. Of course, the man I love and the boy I want to adopt are werewolves. How much weirder can my life possibly get?"

Sally turned when Chase cleared his throat. He was fully clothed in jeans and a T-shirt. "Um, did I hear you say that you were thinking about adopting me? I thought you just wanted to be my foster mom."

"Would that be okay with you?" Sally asked.

Chase rushed forward and hugged her fiercely. "I would love nothing more than for you to be my mom."

"I know I'll never be able to take your mom's place, but I would love to nurture you and watch you grow into the amazing man I see you becoming. You don't have to call me Mom or anything unless you want to. There's no pressure there at all."

"Thank you, Miss Sally. You don't know what that means to me."

CHAPTER 32

"I think they will probably look for your mom in the morning," Sally said. "I imagine this is a daylight type of operation."

"The sheriff's department will want to search and make an official investigation. After they're finished, we can give your mom a proper burial," Jake told Chase as he clapped him on the shoulder.

They were temporarily blinded by headlights as a sheriff's car rolled up to the front of the barn and parked.

"Zeke, it's always good to see you, but I sure have seen a lot of you lately." Jake said.

"Too much, Jake. This is not how I expected to spend my evening. I need for someone to tell me exactly what happened here."

Sally started by telling him how Danny had broken into the house through Chase's bedroom window, prepared to burn the place down. Jake and Chase took turns detailing all of the events that led up to Danny's current condition. By the end of the story, Zeke's eyes were narrowed.

"So, Sally, I take it you believe in ghosts and werewolves?" Zeke asked.

"Yes. It's difficult to refute what I saw firsthand," Sally replied.

"Are you okay with the knowledge, or do I need to erase it from your memory?"

Sally was taken aback. "No! Don't you dare go messing around in my head! I'm happy that I know about Jake and Chase. They mean a lot to me, and knowing that side of them can only help me understand them better."

Zeke smiled. "That's a good answer. Just know that you can't tell anyone of their dual nature. I mean it. We'd have an old-fashioned lynch-mob situation if this information got out."

"Sheriff, I just dealt with a murderer, a ghost, and a werewolf. I have two weapons smugglers gunning for me. Who would believe such a tale? Don't worry, I won't tell anyone."

"Glad to hear it. Now, we need to look for Pam. I'd rather look for her after the sun comes up. Let me make some phone calls. This is a holiday week, so a lot of folks are on vacation. I may not be able to get the equipment here for a few days." He walked to his car to make his calls in private.

He returned a few minutes later. "We're in luck. Plenty of folks were fond of Pam, and I was able to get everyone together. I'll have a team here in the morning to search the back barnyard. Will you all be here?"

"I'm not going anywhere until we find my mom," Chase said sternly.

"I'll be here, too," Jake agreed.

"I will be here, Sheriff. What time should we expect you?" Sally asked.

"It'll probably be around eight o'clock or so. Chase, I don't know if you should really be here for this. It might be best if you found somewhere else to be."

"Zeke, I need to be here," Chase argued.

"Okay. I guess you're man enough to know what you can and can't handle."

"Zeke, I haven't seen any of the people who are supposed to be guarding this place. Shouldn't they have made themselves known by now? I'm worried something has happened to them." Sally wrung her hands together.

"I noticed that when I drove in, and it's worrisome. I have some men looking for those agents and my own men who have failed to check in. I expect to hear something soon."

"Sheriff, I forgot about the cameras when I transformed," Chase said sadly. "They may have caught it."

"Steele is the one manning the camera surveillance, so you'll be fine. Just don't do anything that foolish again."

Zeke's cell phone buzzed and he answered with a curt, "Yeah?" He walked away so they couldn't hear the rest of the conversation.

He returned a moment later. His eyes gleamed like polished steel. "They found four ATF agents unconscious at their posts. Looks like some sort of gas was used. Two of my men are missing. Every camera we installed is smashed. You all need to get back to the house, and I need to take care of Danny. I have someone coming to take the worm to jail. I'll join you once he's out of here."

"Do you think Danny gassed those agents?" Sally asked.

"No. I think the Martinez brothers are here, and our night just got really interesting. Now go!"

"On our way," Jake said taking Sally's hand and leading her back to the house.

CHAPTER 33

Jake searched the house when they returned. "All clear." He double checked all of the door and window locks.

"Jake, what are we going to do?" Sally waved her arms towards the ceiling. "Most of our backup has been taken out of commission. What kind of people can take out that many ATF and sheriff deputies?"

Jake slipped his arms around her. "Sweetness, we are going to get through this. By this time tomorrow, your biggest worry is going to be what to take to Grandma's house for Sunday dinner."

Chase offered her a genuine smile. "Dinner is going to be so good. I bet Mrs. Hill makes homemade hot rolls. She looks like the type of lady to do that. You can take peanut butter cookies as your contribution."

She laughed. "We'll see about that, Chase."

What he might have said was cut off by heavy boots stomping across the porch. Jake opened the door and ushered Zeke inside. He entered the house carrying a large tactical bag and wearing a deadly scowl.

"Any word on your missing men?" Jake asked softly.

"Yeah. They were found unconscious by the creek. Whatever was used to knock them out is unlike anything I've ever seen. We need to consider that the Martinez brothers have a more varied arsenal than we first thought."

"So, are we going to wait for them to come to us or go out looking for them?" Sally asked.

"We'll make our stand here at the house. I take it you have some weapons here?" At Jake's nod, Zeke continued. "Here, take these." He reached into his bag and withdrew four police issue tactical gas masks. He gave one to each of them.

They didn't waste any time in putting the masks on, which covered their eyes, noses and mouths. Sally was adjusting the straps on her mask when she heard the kitchen window break.

"They're here!" Zeke shouted.

Sally pulled her pistol from her pocket while Jake grabbed the rifle by the front door. Chase produced a knife from his pocket, and they rushed into the kitchen.

"It's a gas canister, all right," Zeke whispered. He turned and saw everyone behind him. "Spread out. Everyone, take a room. I'll take the kitchen. They'll be coming in soon."

Chase dashed into his bedroom, but before the rest of them could spread out as instructed, the kitchen door was blown off its hinges with an explosion and flash of light. Smoke filled the house, and two large figures emerged from the haze. They wore gas masks, full Kevlar body armor, and carried automatic weapons, which they pointed at the group in the kitchen.

"Don't anybody move!" the one on the left yelled. He turned to Sally. "We're here to collect what you owe us, bitch."

Sally squared her shoulders and pointed her gun back at

the man. "I don't owe you anything. I don't even know you."

The man on the right laughed. "Look, someone double crossed us. You had our guns, so it must have been you. You're Dale's granddaughter, so it must be in the blood."

"The ATF took the guns. I didn't even know they were there. Wouldn't it make more sense to go after the person who was supposed to have them? He's probably the one who stashed them in my barn. And what does my grandpa have to do with anything? He died years ago."

"Don't play dumb. We don't care who stashed them. They were in your barn. You owe us five million bucks. We'll take it now," the left one snarled. "If you don't have it, your life is ours."

"Are you thinking we should sell her to recoup our loss, Vinnie?"

"I don't think she'd bring near enough money for our trouble, Micah. The dudes are worthless. I say we just kill them all now." He turned his gun on Jake.

There was a blur and Vinnie was abruptly without his weapon. When Sally blinked next, Chase and Vinnie were rolling around on the floor. Before Micah could turn his gun on them, Jake tackled him. It didn't take long before both Jake and Chase had bested their opponents and ripped their masks off. The thugs wheezed a couple times and passed out from the gas they had tossed into the house.

Zeke wasted no time. He nudged Chased aside and handcuffed Vinnie. He tossed a pair of handcuffs to Jake who made quick work of securing Micah. They each hefted a bad guy on their shoulders and carried them to the front porch. They dropped them on the weathered boards with only enough care not to break any bones. Zeke took smelling salts from his pocket and brought both men back to consciousness.

"You are both under arrest for attempted murder, assaulting multiple police officers, property destruction, illegal arms dealing, human trafficking, breaking and entering, and being a couple of assholes," Zeke snarled. He read them their rights. "Is there anything you'd like to say?"

Vinnie curled his lip. "Yeah. You've gone and done it now. Our old man will have something to say about this!"

"I'm sure he will. I plan to have a nice long chat with your father. Let's hope he doesn't join you in your future accommodations." Zeke spoke several police codes into his radio.

Two deputies arrived in squad cars a few minutes later. Zeke handed his prisoners off to them. "I need these two transported separately, and I'll be in to interrogate them soon. I just need to tie up a few loose ends here first."

They nodded and walked the infamous Martinez brothers down the steps and assisted them into their respective cars.

"You probably shouldn't stay here tonight. The air won't be safe to breathe for a while. I recommend you find someplace safe to stay for a day or two while it clears out."

"We have some options. Thanks, Zeke." She hugged herself. "Are you still searching for Pam tomorrow morning, or do you need to postpone that?"

He glanced at Chase before replying. "We will be here around eight o'clock tomorrow morning. Let's see if we can find her. Everyone involved needs closure."

"Thanks, Sheriff. What will happen to Danny if we don't find my mom?"

"He will still be charged with murder. His lawyer might get it lowered to involuntary manslaughter, but he isn't going to walk away from this unscathed." He rested his hand on Chase's shoulder. "Are you okay, son? Do you want me to drop you by Christy's on my way into town?"

"I'm fine, Sheriff. I'll go with Jake and Miss Sally to wherever they're going. Thank you."

"I'll see you all in the morning. Get some rest." So

saying, Zeke sauntered to his car.

Sally stood beside Jake in the open doorway, watching as the sheriff drove a little way up the lane where he stopped and got out of the car to talk to a couple of deputies. They spoke briefly before Zeke climbed back in his patrol car and left.

Jake turned to Sally and Chase. "I'm calling Grandma. I'm sure she'll let us stay with her."

Sally nodded. "Okay. We'll grab some clothes while you call." She and Chase trudged through the house with their masks still firmly in place and gathered the necessities.

When they came back outside, they found Jake talking to the two deputies with whom Zeke had spoken earlier. "Sally and Chase, I'd like you to meet Deputies Walker and Somers. They're going to watch the house tonight and make sure nothing more happens. We need to leave the windows open, so the gas will completely dissipate."

Sally shook their hands and said, "Pleased to meet you, Deputies. Thank you for keeping an eye on things tonight. I really don't feel comfortable leaving the windows open with no one here."

Deputy Walker tipped his hat and replied, "It's all in a day's work for us. Don't worry about anything. Just get some rest."

She climbed in the passenger seat of Jake's truck. She waved to the deputies as Jake slid behind the wheel, and Chase claimed the backseat. They drove away from what was quickly becoming their home in silence.

CHAPTER 34

Mrs. Hill opened the door, a kind smile on her lips. "Come in! Come in! You poor dears have been through so much. Come into the kitchen, and I'll make us all a nice snack."

They all tromped into the kitchen and fell into the chairs at the table. They sat in quiet contemplation for a while before Sally got up and went to Chase. She wrapped her arms around his neck in a tender hug.

"I'm so sorry for your loss. I can't imagine the pain you've suffered. If there's ever anything I can do to take even a tiny bit of that pain away, you just let me know."

Chase patted her arm and said, "Thanks, Miss Sally, but I don't want to talk about it right now."

"Of course. Whenever you are ready to talk, you know where to find me." She let go and trudged back to her chair.

Mrs. Hill brought a plate piled high with cupcakes to the table and then fetched a pitcher of milk. "Here, have a little something to eat. From what Jake said on the phone, you've all had a heck of a night."

"You could say that, Grandma," Jake sighed.

"Well now, I think you should tell me about it." Mrs. Hill sat back in her chair and folded her arms.

Sally's shoulders slumped. "Danny broke into the house and tried to burn it down. Then two thugs knocked out all of the ATF agents and most of the deputies guarding my place before they broke in and demanded I pay them five million dollars for guns that I didn't even know were in my barn until someone set it on fire. One of those scumbags said something I still don't understand, though. He said I was Dale's granddaughter, so double crossing must run in my blood. Do you understand what he meant, Mrs. Hill?"

Her breath whooshed out before she answered. "Oh, my dear Sally Sue, I really thought it would be okay by now. I believed they would have forgotten all about the farm, but it looks like they've been using it this whole time."

"I don't know what you're talking about," Sally cried.

"You really don't know. Do you? Fern told me they were keeping this from you. That's why they left the farm to Frank in the first place. He was tied up in the business, too. Your parents never mentioned why they didn't get the farm upon your grandparents' death? Not once?"

"No. Please tell me what this is all about." Sally fought the tears that burned her throat.

Mrs. Hill reached across the table and took her hand. "Sally Sue, your grandpa was part of an organization in his youth. It was the type of organization that doesn't let you quit or retire. The only way out of the business is death. Even in his older years, he was still forced to transport merchandise to select locations. Are you understanding what I'm telling you, dear?"

The tears overflowed Sally's eyes as she shook her head. "No. I'm so confused. Please spell it out for me."

"I don't know all of the details, but I do know that your grandparents were involved with organized crime. Once they were in, they couldn't get out. They left the farm to

Frank in the hopes that the boss wouldn't turn and go after your parents or you. Frank was a part of the group, too. The organization used the farm for something, and your grandparents knew that Frank would let them continue to do so. They were sure your parents would try to put a stop to it and get killed in the process. They didn't want that."

Sally sat back in her chair with her mouth gaping open. She sputtered a few times, but words wouldn't come out.

Jake leaned his elbows on the table. "You're saying that Sally's grandparents left the farm to Frank to protect her and her parents from professional criminals and no one bothered to tell them?"

"I don't know how much her parents know, but given the fact they move around a lot and mostly stay abroad makes me think they know enough to stay away."

Sally moaned and dropped her head into her hands. She sobbed with great gasps of air and moist hiccups. When the fit finally passed, she looked at Mrs. Hill. "How many more secrets could there possibly be around here? I feel like I've been hit by a bulldozer. No one was who I thought. Please don't tell me that you were involved with them too."

"Oh Heavens, no! I'm merely the neighbor. The organization didn't know that Fern and I were close. I didn't know about any of this until right before they died. They hid it well."

"What do you mean you found out right before they died, Grandma?" Jake whispered. His eyes gleamed with a predatory light.

"Fern came to visit me about a week before their car accident. She told me that they had a will drawn up and were leaving the farm to Frank. When I asked her why and argued that your dad should inherit the place, she told me about the spot they were in. The boss wanted them to make a run of something, but your grandpa had refused. He told the boss that he was too old to be doing that type of work anymore. He wanted to come clean and contact the police. I don't know if they ever told your dad or not."

Sally sat straight up as something occurred to her. "Ma said that my grandparents were good people and sometimes good people do bad things. Do you think Ma knows anything about this?"

Jake nodded solemnly. "I would be willing to bet she does. That woman knows way too much to be in the dark about this."

Chase cleared his throat. "I think you ought to go to talk to Ma, then. Maybe she can help."

"She gave me her cell phone number, but this isn't something that should be discussed on the phone. I need to talk to her about this in person." Sally fisted her hands. "I think I'll go visit her at the diner tomorrow afternoon."

"You're right," Jake growled. "We also need to talk to Zeke. He asked you about an organized crime connection earlier, didn't he?"

"Yes. He told me to have Dad call him when I hear from my parents next." Tears again raced down Sally's cheeks. "Surely my parents aren't involved. They are missionaries! They build schools and churches in third world countries. What am I going to do if they're criminals, too?"

Jake leapt from his seat and gathered Sally in his arms in one smooth motion. "Don't you worry, Sweetness, it will be okay. We'll figure it out, and everything will be okay." He rubbed soothing circles on her back.

Sally leaned into his embrace and rested her weary head on his shoulder. "Thank you."

After a few minutes, she pulled away from him and stood. "Thank you for your hospitality, Mrs. Hill. If it's all right with you, I think I'll go to bed now. Am I in the same room as last time?"

Mrs. Hill shook her head. "Chase is using that room. You are in the room next door to the one you used before."

"I'll walk you up." Jake stood and offered her his hand.

Overwhelmed and exhausted, she held his hand as they walked up the stairs, leaning much of her weight against him.

"I could carry you," Jake whispered in her ear.

"Thanks for the offer, but I'm still capable of climbing stairs."

Jake pushed open the door to the room that his grandmother had indicated and escorted Sally inside. "I guess you realize that we're sharing this room tonight. This means that Grandma has accepted you and our relationship. I know you don't feel like celebrating now, but later you'll see what a big deal this is."

She swayed on her feet. "Yeah, your grandma is a nice lady. I thought mine was, too. I'm going to bed now. Goodnight, Jake." She plopped on the bed in her clothes and shoes. She didn't even bother to get under the covers. She was nearly asleep when she felt Jake remove her shoes, lift her slightly, and pull the blankets over her.

"Goodnight, Sweetness. I love you," he whispered as he feathered a soft kiss across her lips.

CHAPTER 35

They all awoke early the next day and had a quick breakfast with Mrs. Hill who followed them when they returned to the farm. Jake went into the house first to determine if the air was safe to breathe. He came back outside and motioned for the others. "It looks like it's all aired out now. I think it's safe to come inside."

Sally stood in the living room staring out the window at the shed while everyone else talked.

Did Grandpa and Grandma hide contraband in that shed? Did they run drugs? Guns? How did they even get involved in something like that in the first place?

Her unpleasant thoughts were interrupted by a knock on the front door. She opened the door to the sheriff, a group of serious looking officers, and a beautiful Labrador Retriever.

"Good morning, Sally. We're ready to start excavating your back barnyard. Would you like to be present, or should I just let you know what we find?"

"I want to come with you, Sheriff. This is something

that I need to see. I need to be sure that all of the taint is removed from this land." She rubbed the goose bumps on her arms.

"I think we should all go with you, Zeke," Mrs. Hill declared. "Pam's disappearance has haunted us all. She needs to be laid to rest properly."

Sally felt a heavy weight on her chest as they marched to the barn.

If Pam's remains are actually here, then Chase has been within a few miles of his mom the whole time. People kept telling the kid that his mom abandoned him. Poor Chase!

They were about to round the corner of the barn to the back when an older model pickup roared down the driveway. It screeched to a stop in front of the barn. Everyone turned to see who was making such a ruckus and were surprised to see Christy jump down from the driver's seat.

"Have I missed anything?" she asked breathlessly.

"Not yet," Zeke replied. "We're just getting started. Are you sure you want to be here?"

"She was my only sister. Of course, I want to find her!" Christy replied.

"This is our cadaver dog, Lily, and her handler, Joe." Zeke gestured to the dog and person holding her leash.

They resumed their walk to the back of the barn and the cadaver dog went right to work. Lily the yellow Labrador wasted no time. She sniffed around in circles until she found something of interest. She began barking and wouldn't stop until her handler gave her a command.

"This is where we need to dig, Sheriff," Joe stated.

Zeke signaled the waiting heavy equipment operator who inched his way around the barn. The skid-steer moved carefully. The operator dug a few feet down until Joe signaled him to stop. The forensic team took over then. They brushed dirt away and indicated that they had found the body. They took several pictures and measurements.

Zeke wouldn't let any of the family see her. The coroner was contacted, and the body was transferred to the morgue.

After the team and coroner had gone, Zeke approached Christy and Chase carrying a locket. "Christy, Chase, do either of you recognize this locket?"

"That's my mom's locket," Chase said. "She wore it all the time."

"I gave it to her when Chase was born," Christy said. "She never took it off. There should be a baby picture of Chase inside."

Zeke opened the locket to reveal a grinning baby Chase. "I have to take this into evidence, but I'll try to give it back to you as soon as possible, Chase. It'll probably be after Danny's trial, though." Zeke clapped him on the shoulder. "I'm so sorry, son."

"Mom is really gone. She didn't run away. I never believed she did." The young man rubbed his eyes.

Sally wrapped her arms around his waist and whispered, "I'm so sorry. So, so very sorry."

He returned Sally's embrace and held her for a long time. She felt a couple tears fall on her neck but didn't let go to wipe them away.

"Chase," Christy began. "We need to talk about something. Your mama had a life insurance policy. I've been paying the premiums all this time. Once we have a death certificate, you'll be getting quite a bit of money. It's your money, but your guardian has control over it until you turn eighteen. There's something I want you to do. I want you to keep the fact that there's any money at all to yourself. If your father gets word of it, there will be nothing but trouble for you. I think it would be best for you to stay here as originally planned. Maybe you can help Sally out with some expenses like groceries. You eat a lot, my dear."

"I don't understand. Why wouldn't you want me to come back home with you and help you pay bills?"

"Because it's not your job to help me pay bills."

Christy' sleeve fell back revealing a bruise on her wrist, which she quickly covered before continuing. "I know Ray hasn't ever been nice to you. I'm sorry for that. I'm stuck with him, but you aren't."

Chase's voice cracked as he said, "Aunt Christy, I'm sorry for all the strain I've caused you. I know Uncle Ray has given you a hard time for taking me in the way you did."

"Sweet Chase, I should be apologizing to you. I've done my best, but I still came up lacking."

"Would you all like to come up to the house with me?" Sally asked. "You can sit at the kitchen table and talk more comfortably there."

She felt a hand on her shoulder and turned. "I'm going to go on home now. You just let me know if you need anything," Mrs. Hill said and walked toward her car.

"Thank you for everything," Sally called behind her.

They made their way back to the house. Sally led them to the kitchen. As she turned to leave, Chase said, "Wait. I want to talk to you and Aunt Christy about you being my foster mom."

"Sweetie, I think you need to process what's happened to your mother right now. I'm ready to do whatever I need to do for you, but this probably isn't the time to talk about it. You and your aunt need to have a nice long talk where you won't be interrupted. I'm going to run an errand, so you two take all the time you need." She turned and left Chase and Christy to talk in private.

CHAPTER 36

S
he found Zeke and Jake waiting for her on the front porch. "Old Man Martinez paid me a visit last night. In light of what Jake just told me about your family, I don't think you are out of danger yet," Zeke sighed.

"You think he means me harm, too?" Sally sank down onto the porch steps.

"I understand you are going to see Ma at the diner today. Perhaps I should go with you," Zeke said.

"Oh, I don't think that's such a good idea. She told me that she doesn't really like lawmen. I'm afraid she won't tell me anything if you're with me."

"You may be right. I do need to sit down and have a long talk with her, though. That woman knows more about what goes on in this county than any other person."

"I can see that, Sheriff. She knows much, but reveals little. I'm not sure I'll be able to find out anything, but I have to go try." She ran her hands through her hair.

"Sally, I don't want you going alone. I'll go with you," Jake said.

"I need to do this alone. This is my family we're talking about. This is my legacy, my secret legacy to uncover."

Zeke nodded. "I respect that, Sally. Good luck. Be on your guard."

"I will. Thank you. There's no time like the present. Chase and Christy are in the house having long overdue closure. I need answers before I can have my own." She stood and started toward her car. She had taken half a dozen steps before she felt Jake behind her and turned.

"I know you have to do this alone, but at least let me go along for the ride. Please. Let me be there for you, Sweetness," he whispered.

"Okay, you can come along for the ride, but this is my show." She poked her finger into his powerful chest.

He chuckled. "Your show. Got it. Do I at least get to drive?"

Sally relaxed her shoulders for the first time all day. "Yeah, you can drive. I'd rather use your gas, anyway."

Jake laughed as he took her hand and led her to his truck. "I love that you are so practical."

The drive was over before Sally realized it. Lost in her tumultuous thoughts, she hadn't spoken a single word to Jake since they got in the truck. It was time to stop thinking and start doing. She looked over at the man who had come to mean the world to her in such a short time.

"Thanks for driving me here. I need to go in by myself, though. Do you mind waiting in the truck?"

"Not at all. Just keep my number pulled up on your phone and call me if you need me. I'll be right here waiting for you."

She leaned over and kissed him lightly before hopping out of the truck and marching inside.

Ma met her at the door. "I'm happy to see that yer okay. I wondered if you'd come see me. I don't s'pose yer here for the coffee?"

Sally shook her head. "I love your coffee, but I need

something else this time."

Ma nodded and motioned for one of her employees to take over hostess duty. "I figured as much. Come back to my office where it's private."

Sally followed her into a small, cluttered office with so much character that it could only belong to Ma. She made herself comfortable in a bright orange rolling chair that had to be from the sixties while Ma settled into her worn leather office chair behind the small wooden desk. The faded daisy wallpaper spoke volumes about Ma's past.

"What can I do for you, Bunny?"

"I learned something upsetting last night. I came to you to see if it's true and if you can give me any more information." Sally picked at the hem of her green sweater nervously.

"What do ya need to know?" Ma asked softly.

A tear escaped her control as she asked, "Were my grandparents part of the mob?"

Ma's expression froze in shock for a moment. "Where did ya hear such a thing?"

"My source is someone I trust, but that doesn't mean the information is accurate. I need to know the truth, Ma. In the past month I've had my barn set on fire. My house has been broken into twice. Danny threatened me on multiple occasions and then attempted to set fire to my house and slit my throat. The feds found military weapons in my barn. A couple of goons threatened my life and discussed selling me into slavery after demanding five million dollars from me because I'm Dale's granddaughter and must be a double crosser. To top it all off, we found Chase's mom's body buried behind the barn this morning. I really need you to be straight with me, Ma. I'm tired of wading through this blind."

Ma took a deep breath and blew it out slowly. She rose from her desk and opened a cabinet behind her. She removed a bottle of whiskey and two highball glasses. She splashed a generous amount of the amber liquid in each glass before returning to the desk and setting one glass in front of Sally while keeping the other.

"So many secrets, Bunny. I'm afraid you've had way too much kept from ya. Let me tell ya a story. A long time ago, two brothers were young and dumb. They were full of testosterone and believed themselves invincible. They had a friend from outta town who told 'em they could make some serious cash by doing just a few little jobs for some people with deep pockets." She took a healthy sip of her whiskey. "They were all about easy money as most young men are. They jumped right on those jobs and asked no questions."

"Grandpa and Uncle Frank?"

"Yep. Now hush and listen. The jobs were easy at first. They just took packages from one place to another, and their payment was left in places like bus station lockers. It was a lot of money, so they kept doin' it. Soon, the boss wanted to meet these two boys who did such a good job. Before they knew it, they were driving getaway cars and things that you don't need to know about."

She took another sip of whiskey before continuing. "While I broke up with Frank when I found out, Fern was sure the boys could get outta the business and went ahead and married Dale. She got sucked in, too. They tried to get out for years and years. When they bought the farm, they thought they could hide. Nope. The boss found 'em and demanded to use the place as a stash house. They'd bring smuggled goods to the farm, let the heat die down, and then collect 'em a bit later. That's exactly what was supposed to happen with those guns in your barn, I'm sure. How old did those cases look?"

"They had been there for a few months, maybe. There wasn't nearly enough dust on them to be something Grandma and Grandpa were involved in."

"I honestly didn't know that yer grandparents left the farm to Frank willingly, but it makes sense now. I 'spect he kept the farm to maintain the stash house. It looks like Danny followed the family footsteps, but somethin' went wrong. He's not the sharpest tool in the shed."

Sally let out a short bark of laughter. "No. He's not the sharpest tool at all."

Ma sobered once again. "Dale told the boss that he was finished when you was a youngster and pert near walked in on a collection. He refused to be a part of the business anymore. He didn't want that evil to touch his little angel. I think that's why he and Fern died. They was run off the road in broad daylight, and I think it was a hit."

Sally processed this information and instinctively reached for the whiskey in front of her. She didn't care that it wasn't even noon yet. She downed the glass in one gulp. The burn of the liquor soothed her frazzled nerves.

"Would you be willing to share this information with the sheriff?" Sally asked.

"No. Bunny, they would kill me and destroy my business. They may do that anyway if they find out I talked to ya 'bout this. I told ya all of this so ya can make sense of things. They never intended for ya to have the farm because they knew that the organization would force ya into a life ya didn't want. Same with yer parents. They're peaceable people. They don't want none of that life of crime. I really thought enough time had passed that you'd be safe. Danny never has any money, so I thought it all ended with Frank."

"Thank you for telling me." Sally stood. "Now I just have to figure out how to keep them off my land and out of my life. Because I'm not about to join them."

Ma smiled broadly. "Good luck, Bunny. If ya need a place to hide, ya got my number."

"Thanks, Ma. Hiding isn't what I have in mind, though. And thanks for the drink. I needed that." She left the office and closed the door softly behind her.

CHAPTER 37

S he was halfway to the truck when a car came screaming toward her out of nowhere. She dove to the side and saw the driver clear as day as the car raced past her. Jake was by her side an instant later helping her up off the pavement.

"It was Ray. I saw him. He just tried to kill me," Sally panted.

The car came around for another attempt. Jake picked her up, threw her over his shoulder, and ran to his truck. He was opening the driver's door when they heard a gunshot. They looked up in time to see one of Ray's tires had been shot out, and Ma was standing just outside the diner door with a rifle in her hands. Jake shoved Sally in the truck.

"Call Zeke and tell him what happened. I'm sure the city police will get involved in this, but we want him to be here as quick as possible." Jake slammed the truck door and ran with inhuman speed toward the car that had just wrapped itself around a light pole.

Sally watched Jake jerk Ray out of the car and argue

while the phone rang. When Zeke answered, she explained everything that had just happened.

"I'll be right there. I'm calling a buddy of mine with the River Falls Police Department. Hopefully, he can beat anyone else there. Stay put, Sally."

She reached over and locked the truck doors as she watched Jake and Ray yell in each other's faces. She could see Jake vibrating with rage and worried that his wolf would show itself. Ma stood by, still holding her rifle, and a small crowd gathered in the parking lot.

She heard sirens in the distance and soon the lot was swarming with people. Police officers, fire fighters, and a tow truck driver mixed with the bystanders. The police interviewed witnesses while the fire fighters and tow truck driver worked at freeing the car, which Sally recognized as Christy's. She unlocked the truck and slid out when she saw an officer approach her.

"Ms. Wagner, I presume?"

"Yes, that's me."

"I'm Detective Shawn Wilson. The sheriff called and asked me to handle your interview."

"Thank you, Detective. I'm not sure where to start," Sally stammered.

"Start with when you saw the car coming. Was it traveling at a high rate of speed or proceeding slowly as one should in a parking lot?"

She took a deep breath and gathered her thoughts. "I was walking out of the diner. I was about halfway through the parking lot when I heard his engine roar. I looked up and saw a black Ford barreling right for me like a bat out of hell. I dove to the side and he missed me. My boyfriend saw it all from his truck. He jumped out and had just helped me up when we saw the car coming back around to try again. That's when Ma shot the tire, and the car crashed. She saved my life, Detective."

He glanced up from his notes with a slight grin. "That

doesn't surprise me at all, Ms. Wagner. So, do you know the suspect?"

"Yes, his name is Ray Jones. His nephew, Chase, has been staying with me. Ray is horrible to him. He's better off with me, so I'm going to try to adopt him."

"I see. Do you think that's a motive for him trying to run you down?"

"I don't know. I wouldn't think so. He doesn't like Chase, so he should be happy that the boy has moved in with me."

"Have you had any heated discussions or disagreements with the suspect?" Detective Wilson asked.

"No. We've never really talked at all other than to be introduced. I see him around town now and then, but we've never so much as discussed the weather."

"Sally, are you all right?" Zeke's booming voice echoed through the parking lot as he walked up behind them.

"Yes, Zeke, I'm okay. He scared me pretty bad, but I'm alive." She gave him a small smile.

"Wilson, thank you for taking care of this for me," Zeke said turning to the detective.

His lips split into a huge smile as he extended his hand for a friendly shake. "Zeke, how the heck are you?"

"Doin' well. How are you?"

"Can't complain. Unlike your little friend here. This gal nearly met her maker today."

"I'm glad he missed. Sally is a real treasure. There's always room in our little community for a spirited woman like her. It doesn't hurt that she makes Jake happy, too." Zeke patted her shoulder.

"Jake is the boyfriend you mentioned?" Detective Wilson asked.

"Yes, Jake was helping me up when Ray spun around for a second shot at me," Sally said in a small voice.

"Well, hell. I'm surprised that guy is still breathing if it was Jake that yanked him out of the car." The detective shook his head.

Zeke replied, "Jake has mellowed over the years, but considering Sally was the target, I am surprised he's still in one piece, too."

Detective Wilson looked at Sally. "Do you have anything you want to add to the official report?"

"No, I think we've pretty much covered everything," Sally replied.

Zeke said, "We're all done here, Sally. I'm sure Jake is anxious to get you to himself. Let's go find him, and then I'll coordinate with Wilson to interrogate Ray."

They found Jake and Ma talking a few feet from the front door. Her lips were flattened in a straight line, and she still clutched her rifle like she was expecting more trouble. She ran to Sally and wrapped her in a fierce hug as Jake and Zeke had a quiet word together. Zeke walked off as Ma began her questioning.

"Bunny, are you okay? Are you hurt anywhere?"

"I'm fine, Ma. Thank you for shooting out Ray's tire. You saved my life. I will be forever in your debt," Sally whispered as she pulled away.

Jake slipped his arm around Sally's shoulders and brought her into the safety of his embrace. He kissed her temple as she looked at Ma.

Ma shook her head. "Damn shame my aim was off, but yer welcome. I'm happy yer okay."

She smiled at Ma's answer. "Your aim may have been off, but you still stopped him. I don't want to know which part of the target you aimed for."

"No, Bunny, I'm sure you don't." Ma chuckled. "Well, now that the excitement is over, I'm gonna get back ta runnin' my diner. I think you two should get back home, but be careful. No tellin' what's gonna jump out at ya next."

"You're right. We'll be careful," Jake answered. "Thanks, Ma. I owe you one."

She grinned. "Don't you forget it either, slick." She went into the diner and closed the door behind her.

Jake pulled Sally fully into his arms and kissed her deeply. His tongue explored as his arms banded around her keeping her safely flush with his body. He pulled away and looked intensely into her eyes.

"I thought I'd lost you, and it scared me. I don't ever want to feel like that again."

"Well, it wasn't a pleasant experience for me, either. Let's go home, Jake. I just want to go home." Sally rested her head on his shoulder.

"Home. Yeah, that's sounds real good, Sweetness." He led her to the truck, opened her door, lifted her in, and then fastened her seat belt as if she was the most precious thing in the world. When he was finished with all that, he feathered the barest hint of a kiss across her lips.

"Tease," she said playfully.

"Not a tease. Just an appetizer. The main course is yet to come," Jake growled.

CHAPTER 38

The drive home was uneventful and quick. When they pulled up in front of the house, she pointed at several vehicles parked there.

"What do you suppose this is all about?" Sally asked.

"One way to find out. Let's go see." He climbed out and was at her side to help her out of the truck by the time she got the door open.

Walking beside him into the house, they were greeted by several of their friends and neighbors. The noise of so many people talking at once was deafening.

Martha shouted, "Quiet!" and the noise fell away.

"We all heard what happened," Mrs. Hill said.

"Yeah, we heard Uncle Ray tried to kill you, Miss Sally. I'm glad you're okay," Chase said softly.

Sally hugged him. "Thank you, Chase. I am, too."

Martha said, "We've all come together to celebrate your survival tonight. Since you've moved here, you have faced more danger and opposition than one person should have to face in a lifetime. So, we decided to do what we could for you. We decided to make you a good meal and take care of the two of you. The food is on the table, and we'll be doing the cleanup afterward. We also installed new glass in the broken window and replaced your damaged kitchen door. We did a few other little things while we were here, too. We want you to know that you are welcome here."

Sally looked around her in amazement. She didn't even know her next-door neighbor's name in the city. He was just Bicycle Guy in her mind because he rode his bicycle every morning before work. She wasn't even moved in yet, and these people were already being good neighbors.

"Aunt Christy wanted to be here, but she's at the jail right now. I'm not sure what she's doing there, but I hope she isn't trying to bail out Uncle Ray." Chase stared at his feet. "You know she didn't have anything to do with him trying to run you over, right?"

"Of course, we know that. Christy is a good person, and I know she'd never be a party to such a thing. Don't worry. We don't blame her." Sally kissed his cheek.

She gasped as she walked into the kitchen and saw the spread. They had everything from meatloaf to chicken soup. "This all looks amazing. Thank you!"

Turning her attention to the rest of her guests she said, "I can't tell you how much we appreciate this. We don't want all this good food getting cold. Let's eat." They ate, drank, and enjoyed the company of everyone there.

Shortly after the last guest left, Sally's cell phone rang. "Hello?"

"Hey, Sally. It's Zeke. Is Jake with you?"

"Yes. Would you like to speak with him?"

"Yes, but I'd like to talk to you both at the same time. Would you put me on speaker? You'll both be interested in this news."

Sally pressed the speaker button and said, "Okay, Zeke, we can both hear you now."

"Good. I just wanted to let you know that Ray confessed

to stealing that weapons shipment from the Martinez brothers who are the main lieutenants of the organization around here. He duped Danny into letting him hide it in the barn."

"So, Danny did know about it! Is he the one who set the barn on fire?" Sally cried.

"Yeah. He was attempting to burn the evidence. He's really not very bright. He thought everything would go up in smoke, and he'd walk away."

"That sounds like Danny. He never did think things completely through." Sally sighed.

"Ray said the same thing. The plan was to wait until the brothers were out of the country, then retrieve the shipment, and smuggle it into Mexico. They could've made some serious cash, but the brothers decided to stay stateside for a while. Danny got antsy every time they almost had things coordinated. As a result, someone tied to the organization would get suspicious and nose around town before they could move the shipment."

"So, he tried to get rid of me because he was afraid I'd find the weapons." Sally sagged against the wall.

"When I told Danny that Ray had spilled the beans, he started singing like a canary. He named names, gave addresses, and told us where to find other stash houses in the area. He even implicated Old Man Martinez as the area crime boss. Says he'll testify against all of them if we will reduce his charges. He's hoping to get a plea deal in Pam's murder, too."

"You can't get a much better confession than that," Jake rumbled. "Did he say what the gas was that they used to knock everyone out?"

"No. He doesn't know about the gas, but if his information proves accurate, we may be able to take down the whole organization, or at least its branch here."

"That's wonderful news!" Sally exclaimed. "Does that mean that I should be able to lead a normal life?"

"Yes. And Sally? He even told us who was driving the car that ran your grandparents off the side of the cliff. It was Old Man Martinez himself. He was still an enforcer then. He wanted to make a name for himself. I'm sorry that's how it happened, but I thought you'd want to know."

"Thanks, Zeke. I'd rather know the truth than live with the questions." She wiped the tears running down her face.

"Well, I'll let you two get some rest."

"Thanks, Zeke. I'm beat."

"Martha said she left enough food to feed an army at your place tonight. At least you won't have to cook for a few days."

"Yeah, they really fixed us up, and I'm eternally grateful," Jake said. "We're going to get off of here now and get some sleep. We've earned it today."

"You're right. Goodnight, lovebirds."

"Goodnight, Zeke," Sally replied and hit the end button on her phone.

CHAPTER 39

S waying with weariness, Sally started toward the bedroom. Jake came up behind her, swept her off her feet, and carried her to bed. He carefully sat her on the edge of the bed and got down on one knee.

"Sally, you are the most important person in my life, and we've already wasted so much time. I don't want to waste another minute. I love you with all of my heart now and forever."

He reached into his pocket and withdrew a small square red velvet box. "I would be honored if you would agree to be mine forever. Sally Sue Wagner, Sweetness, will you marry me?"

She flung her arms around his neck and squealed, "Yes, I will marry you!"

He slipped a sparkling princess cut engagement ring on her finger, the center stone standing proudly surrounded by small round cut diamonds set in a white gold band. Then he kissed her soundly. He pulled away when he heard the knock on the bedroom door.

"Do you need something, Chase?" Jake called.

"Can I come in for a minute?"

"Of course," Sally answered.

The door eased open and Chase stood awkwardly in the doorway. He stared at them for a moment before he stepped into the room. "So, you're getting married?"

"Yes," Sally answered with a smile that lit her whole face. "Look at this beautiful ring that Jake bought for me." He offered her a tiny smile. "It's pretty. Congratulations." He stared at them a moment more before he said, "I have a question."

"What is it, Chase?" Jake asked softly.

"With everything that's happened and now you getting married, do you still want me? Things have changed. Uncle Ray's in jail. Danny and the Martinez brothers won't bother you again. So, I just wondered where I fit." He ran his toe over a seam in the floor and wouldn't look at them.

"Of course, we still want you," Jake said standing up. He walked over to the boy and wrapped him in a warm hug. "That hasn't changed. It just means that I'm going to be your dad if we can work the adoption out. And I mean adoption, not foster care. Don't ever think we don't want you."

"My dad?" A myriad of emotions crossed the youngster's face before he simply said, "Okay then. Goodnight." He closed the door softly behind him.

Sally had tears in her eyes as she gazed at her fiancé. "That was perfect. Absolutely perfect."

"No. This is perfect." Jake wrapped her in his arms and pulled her onto the bed where he held her in the safety of his embrace until morning.

Sally decided to attend church that Sunday. She walked into the old whitewashed wooden church where her grandparents had worshipped during their lives. The sermon was as she expected, but she was shocked when Mrs. Hill walked up to the pulpit.

"I would like to thank the Good Lord for my grandson who is newly engaged to the most enchanting, strong, and intelligent woman I've ever met. I look forward to officially welcoming her into my family. I also look forward to welcoming my future great-grandchild, Chase. I'm thankful for the family the three of them have formed."

The congregation applauded, but the elderly woman wasn't finished.

"I'm thankful the organized crime presence that has plagued our area for so many years is being dismantled and the criminals will be standing trial for their crimes. I'm thankful that Pam's disappearance has finally been solved, and her killer will know justice."

The church came alive with parishioners shouting "Amen" and "Praise God" before Mrs. Hill continued.

"One person brought about all of these events. Sally Sue Wagner made it all possible. She has come home to us, and I would like for the entire congregation to embrace her as one of our own."

Sally felt her face flaming, but she couldn't let Mrs. Hill down after that beautiful speech. She stood and addressed the congregation. "I would like to thank you all for your hospitality, and I look forward to forging relationships, old and new, and a new legacy of kindness and truth. No more secrets."

CHAPTER 40

People gathered for Pam's memorial service and filled the little country church to capacity. Sally couldn't see an inch of extra pew space, all of the folding chairs were in use, and people were standing along the walls.

Chase sat in the front pew with Christy and her kids. His shoulders were straight, and his mouth was set in a grim line. It was the expression in his eyes when he turned to look at her that tore at Sally's heart, though. They were dry, but they were the saddest eyes she'd ever seen. He held the same stoic facial expression throughout the service.

When the reverend dismissed the crowd to walk to the nearby cemetery, Chase followed the casket without looking at anyone. The reverend led everyone in prayer and then was about to dismiss the crowd when Chase stood. There was a collective gasp as he walked up to stand beside the reverend.

"If you don't mind, sir, I would like to say something." Moisture finally gathered in his rapidly reddening eyes.

The reverend patted his shoulder. "By all means, my child, you go right ahead and speak your piece."

Chase searched the crowd until his eyes found Sally. "I lost my mom six years ago. Most folks believed she'd left me. I knew better. She was a great mom. She protected me, loved me, and made me laugh. But she was taken away from me."

Sally wiped the tears from her eyes, but for a moment couldn't catch her breath.

"Now we know what happened to her. We know a lot of things. We know she was a good mom. She wanted the best for me. We know my fake dad and my real dad are both in jail. Mom never intended for any of this to happen, but it did. I miss her, but I think she's smiling down from Heaven right now because I have a new mom and dad who love me. I'm pretty sure a good family is all she ever wanted for me." He nodded to the crowd and went back to his seat.

Silence filled the truck cab on the drive home from Pam's service. Sally was at a loss for what to say to her sweet boy. He'd been through so much and yet found it within himself to be grateful.

"Chase, I want you to know that I love you. What you said today at the cemetery was beautiful and heartbreaking at the same time." She reached into the backseat and covered his hand with hers.

"Thank you, Miss Sally." He studied her for a moment. "Can I ask you something?"

"You can ask me anything."

"Is it too soon to call you 'Mom'?" He stared at his shoes.

"It's not too soon for me, but I don't want to rush you. You can call me 'Mom' when you're ready. Your heart will tell you when it's time." She fought the fresh tears that threatened to spill.

"I'd like to start now." He took a deep breath. "Mom. I haven't called anyone that in six years." He furrowed his brow.

"Does it feel right?" Sally patted his hand. "There's really no pressure to change that if you're not ready."

"Yeah, it does." He looked up at her. "What about Jake?"

She laughed. "I'd rather not have Jake call me 'Mom.' I think it would sound weird coming from my fiancé."

"No. I mean, do I have to wait until you're married to call him 'Dad'?"

Jake parked the truck in the driveway and turned to Chase. "You can call me whatever you like unless it's insulting. You don't have to wait until after the wedding unless you want to."

"Dad. Pop. Papa. Father." Chase tested each moniker. "I like 'Dad.'"

Jake smiled and his eyes sparkled with joy. "I like it, too."

"Dad, when are you and Mom getting married, anyway?"

"We've been wanting to talk to you about that. We need to choose our wedding party and be sure everyone is available. Sally's parents will take time to reach, but I have a buddy searching for them. We're thinking this spring would be a good time. What do you think?"

Chase nodded. "Spring is a good time. Are you going to be married at the church?"

"We haven't decided yet, but it will be close." Sally smiled. "This is home now."

"Chase, I need a best man." Jake held his gaze.

"Oh, well, maybe Zeke would want to do it. Have you asked him?"

"We had someone else in mind," Sally said.

"Chase, would you please honor us by being our best man?" Jake's formal question startled the boy.

"Me?" His face brightened and a smile tugged at his lips. "I think I can work that into my busy schedule."

CHAPTER 41

"Come in, Christy. Have a seat and be comfortable. How are you doing?" Sally motioned toward an easy chair facing the Christmas tree.

Christy sighed as she sank into the oversized chair. She closed her sunken eyes briefly before she answered. "I will be okay. Ray is being stubborn about the divorce. He says he doesn't want me out whoring around while he's in jail. After him, why in the world would I ever want to deal with another man?"

"What an ass! What are you going to do?" She eased into the chair next to Christy and studied the new lines on her friend's pale face.

"Detective Wilson from River Falls offered to talk to him for me. He said he thought he could make him see reason. I don't like involving others in my business, but I'm so tired that I don't know how much fight I have left in me. I feel like Ray has sucked all the life right out of me. He sucked all of the money out of our joint accounts, too."

"I'm so sorry. I didn't realize you knew Detective Wilson that well, though. He seems like a decent guy."

"I don't know him, really. Zeke introduced us when I went to visit Ray in jail the first time. They were doing paperwork from the arrest." Her sleeve fell back when she reached up to tuck a lock of silver-streaked black hair behind ear, revealing a fading bruise that looked like a thumbprint.

"Yes, I understand they're pretty good friends." Sally stared at the bruise, but she didn't seem to notice.

Christy pulled her sleeve back down and continued. "Anyway, I ran into him at Ma's Diner when I was in River Falls meeting with my lawyer a few days ago. He asked if he could join me, and before I knew what I was doing, I had told him about all of my troubles. He ended up offering to talk to Ray and buying my lunch."

"That was nice of him. I'm sure he would be a good guy to have on your side."

"I need all the good guys I can get on my side. I feel like someone has taken my life and hacked it into a million pieces. I'm scrambling to try to find them all and put them back together. The kids want their daddy, and I'm praying he rots in jail for what he did. The bastard keeps telling me he'll be out in no time. Either way, we're getting divorced. Thanks to him, I may have to sell my farm." She sank back into the chair like a deflated beach ball.

"Ray has to know he can't beat the attempted vehicular homicide charges. He might get out of the illegal weapons charge, but there were tons of witnesses to him trying to kill me."

"Sally, I'm so sorry he tried to kill you." Christy wiped the tears from her cheeks. "And he did it with my car. If he hadn't wrecked it, I would have been the prime suspect. Shawn thinks he did that on purpose."

"Shawn?"

"Detective Wilson. I'm sorry. He insisted I call him

Shawn. Anyway, he said that since I'm the first driver listed on the insurance for that car, they would have looked at me as the prime suspect. He thinks Ray was setting me up to take the fall."

"Like I said, Ray's an ass. I hope the detective can make him see reason and convince him to agree to the divorce." Sally patted her shoulder.

"Thanks. Me, too. I shouldn't have stayed with him so long. I was raised that you were supposed to marry for life. Divorce was not supposed to be an option. Sally, you have no idea how awful that man became over the years. I thought I loved him because we had great chemistry. I was too young to realize that marriage had to be based on more than that. Marrying him was my greatest mistake." She covered her face with her hands.

Sally stood and searched around for some way to comfort her. "Would you like a drink? I have regular and diet cola and sweet tea."

Christy moved her hands and smiled. "Sweet tea would be great. Thank you."

She was staring at the Christmas tree when Sally returned with their drinks. "You didn't invite me here to discuss my problems, I'm sure. What's on your mind?"

Sally took a quick sip of her tea before answering. "I do have a question I'd like to ask you, but the timing isn't the best. Please feel free to say no if you aren't up to it."

Christy tilted her head and lifted her brows. "Whatever you need, just consider it done."

She ran her palms up and down the legs of her jeans a few times before meeting Christy's gaze. "I'm so sorry about the timing, but I really want to ask you. None of my other friends will understand what a miracle this is. As you know, Jake and I are getting married this spring."

"Yes. Do you need me to help with the decorations or something?"

"Well, yes. That isn't what I want to ask you, though.

Would you stand up with me and be my matron of honor?"

Christy leapt to her feet with a screech. "Yes! I'd be proud to stand up for you and Jake. I've never been anybody's matron of honor before. That means I'm your go-to for all the wedding stuff, right?"

"Yeah. You don't have to do this if you don't feel up to it, though."

"I'm honored you asked me. Your wedding is a testament to what love can accomplish. You and Jake had so many obstacles thrown at you. You were separated before you even had a chance to get together. Then you butted heads when you finally found each other again. But you did, and now you're building a life together. Being part of this is the best thing I can imagine."

Sally smiled and hugged her. "Thank you so much! We have a ton to do, and I don't know where to start. I need a cake, dress, bouquet, music, a venue, and I don't even know what else."

CHAPTER 42

C hristy stood up straight and her lips lifted at the corners in the first true smile Sally had seen from her. "Well, I'm here to help you now. We got this! We can start making a list now if you want. Do you have some paper and a pen?"

"I do. Let's go to the kitchen. Would you like some peanut butter cookies?"

Christy laughed. "That sounds good."

Sally took a pad of paper and a pen from a drawer and grabbed the cookie jar from the top of the refrigerator.

Christy snagged the pen and paper and labeled the top, "Sally and Jake are Finally Getting Married List."

"Okay." Sally rubbed her hands together and smiled. "This doesn't feel so daunting now. Do you know of a good bakery for the cake?"

"Beth's Bakery in Elderberry is worth a visit. Her operation is small, but she's wicked talented. She's close, too, so she might even deliver depending on where you have the wedding. Then there are a few places in River

Falls we can check out."

"Can you call her and arrange a tasting for me?"

"I'd be happy to. She's an old friend from school. It'll be nice to see her in her element. Next."

"Music. I have no idea about music."

"Do you want live music or a recording?"

"Live, I guess. But not a whole band. Maybe one violin or something."

Christy scratched her head. "I don't know any musicians, but I'll ask around and see what I can come up with. Next."

"Venue." Sally ran her fingers through her hair. "I want to get married here locally, but I don't know if the church can hold everyone. Jake and I are inviting over a hundred people. Is there a place around here that you know of?"

Christy smiled and cocked her head. "Have you considered getting married here?"

"Isn't that what I just said?"

"No, I mean here on the farm. In the front yard. We can plant some flowers and put up a few decorations. We could pretty up the place real nice. What do you think?"

Sally laughed and clapped her hands. "That's brilliant! It will save us some money, too. Always a good thing. You're really good at this, Christy!"

She grinned. "Thanks. Next?"

"I need a photographer. I don't even know where to look for one." She shrugged her shoulders.

"My cousin, Lizzy, is a photographer. She's good, but she's just starting her business. She's recently divorced and could really use the money and a good reference. She was in a partnership with her ex-husband where they travelled to schools and churches taking portraits, but the judge gave him the business. She can't use the name or try to contact any of the clients."

"I like the idea of using someone who really needs the business." Sally tapped a finger on her chin. "I'd be happy to talk to her."

"I can set up a meeting with her if you like."

Sally nodded. "That would be great. So, I guess we should talk about the dress. I don't want a white one. I wore a gorgeous white gown with tons of ruffles and beads when I married my first husband. I don't want this wedding to resemble that one at all."

"Okay. That means we can have a lot of options. We aren't limited to dresses sold purely as wedding gowns. Do you have any idea of what style you might want?"

"Nothing too fancy. I don't want to look like Cinderella at the ball."

Christy laughed. "No Cinderella. Got it. There's a little shop in River Falls that specializes in western wear called Down Home Fancy Duds. The owner makes a lot of square dance dresses. Since you're having an outdoor wedding, would you consider a country kind of dress? Maybe with cowboy boots instead of heels?"

"I love that idea! I could pick out the boots, and she could design a dress to match. Oh, that's perfect! I can't thank you enough for all of this help. You are a gem, my friend."

Christy looked at her watch. "They're open for a few more hours today. Do you want to go see what they can do?"

"Oh, yeah. I'll drive." Sally pulled on her jacket and took her purse from its hook on the wall.

"Have you thought about flowers?" Christy asked as Sally merged onto the highway.

"Not really. I guess I may as well make that decision today too. Grandma used to have these pretty purple irises when I was a kid. I keep thinking about those flowers. What do you think about planting some more of those and having living plants instead of cut flowers as decorations?"

"I think that's a great idea," she said making notes on her paper. "Are you going to have purple as a wedding color then?"

Sally thought for a minute and then nodded. "Yes. I like purple. I think pale yellow and various shades of purple. Like I can have my dress be one shade of purple and your dress be another. Then we'll carry bouquets with a few different shades in them. We can accent with yellow. Oh, this is fun!"

Christy shook her head. "Silly, Sally. It's supposed to be fun."

Thirty minutes later, they parked in front of the converted house that served as a western wear shop and catered to square dancers. A petite older woman with bouncy gray curls met them at the door.

"Welcome to Down Home Fancy Duds! I'm Becky. How can I help you today?"

"Hi. I'm Sally, and I'm hoping you can help me with a wedding dress."

Becky's finely lined face fell. "Sweetie, I'm sorry, but I don't sell wedding dresses. I sell dancing dresses. There's a David's Bridal on Central Street."

Christy sprang into action. "She doesn't want a typical wedding dress. She wants something special with down home flair. I thought we could talk to you about designing something similar to a dancing dress, but just a bit more formal."

"Yes, I'm going to wear cowboy boots, and I'd like those to be visible. Maybe a tea-length dress in purple?" Sally leaned closer and held her breath.

Becky studied her for a moment. "Let's see what we can come up with then. Right this way."

They spent the next two hours looking at popular dance dress designs and noting what they liked and what they didn't. After they had gone through her dress book and chose a fabric, Becky began sketching. She sketched a few different styles and then Sally pointed to one and squealed.

"That's it! That is my perfect dress!"

Becky smiled broadly. "How soon do you need it?"

"Four months," Sally said. "Is that enough time?"

"Honey, I'll have it done by Valentine's Day. That way you'll have plenty of time for fittings and alterations. Now, let's find some boots, so we can match the color."

They left Down Home Fancy Duds with springs in their steps. Sally turned to Christy once they were in the car. "This is really going to happen. I'm marrying the love of my life, and everything is finally falling into place. Thank you."

"It's my pleasure. Now, we just have to handle food, tables, chairs, candelabras . . ."

She laughed. "I get the idea, Christy. The important stuff is under control."

"Yeah, the rest is all small potatoes. No sweat."

CHAPTER 43

S ally paced the airport lobby outside the TSA checkpoint for the umpteenth time. She checked her watch again. The plane had been on the ground for thirty minutes. She smoothed her hands down her skirt with unsteady fingers.

"Sally!"

She whirled around to see her mother running toward her. Her mom's hiking boots made clomping sounds with every step, her silver hair and light pink sweater flapped in the breeze she created. Sally opened her arms just in time to stop the tiny woman's momentum.

"Sally, look at you! You look fabulous! I missed you so much!" Her mom gushed as tears reddened her hazel eyes.

"Mom, it's good to see you, too. How was your flight? Where's Dad?"

"Your father is waiting for our luggage. I couldn't wait to see you, so I left him to it. How are you, my sweet girl?"

"I'm doing well considering all the wedding stress. I'm so glad you're here to help me with all of this, Mom. I'm in

229

over my head. My matron of honor is frantically searching for a new musician because the one we booked has the flu. The caterer keeps telling me what I ordered isn't available, and then the next thing I order isn't available. And I'm getting married tomorrow! It's madness!"

"It will all work out. You will be such a beautiful bride. So, this Jake is the same one that was your friend when you were little, right?"

"Yes. We reconnected when I bought Grandma and Grandpa's farm."

"Sally, you look well." The deep baritone voice could only belong to the hulking older man hurrying to her. His sandy blonde hair was barely streaked with silver, and his keen brown eyes had lost none of their luster.

"Dad, it's good to see you." Sally gave him an awkward one-armed hug.

"Congratulations on your pending nuptials." George Wagner boomed.

"Thanks, Dad."

"Well, now that you have our luggage, let's get out of here. I've been breathing recycled air for the past day and a half. I'm ready for fresh air and sunshine." Sally's mom grasped the handles of one of the suitcases and rolled it toward the door.

They made quick work of loading Sally's car and getting underway. The drive from the airport to Sally's place was an hour and a half, so they had plenty of time to talk.

Sally bit her lip and tapped her thumbs on the steering wheel as she merged onto the highway. "I was worried you two wouldn't make it to the wedding. It had been so long since I'd heard from you."

Her dad ran a hand through his shaggy hair and shook his head. "I'm sorry we haven't been in touch. We were building schools in Somalia. Things got dangerous, and we had to be cautious. We didn't realize so much time had passed. One day blurred into another. We were shocked when Jake's Air Force friend tracked us down."

"It may be time to stay home for a while," her mom said.

"You may be right, Tammy. I could use a rest." George rubbed the back of his neck.

Sally's shoulders tensed as she prepared to ask the questions burning a hole in her heart. "Did you know about Grandma and Grandpa? Did you know about Uncle Frank and Danny? Did you know about the organization?"

George turned in his seat to face her. His ruddy face was shiny with a layer of sweat, and his brows were puckered. "We knew there was a connection, but we never had any details. They kept me away from all that. It was never supposed to touch you. What in the name of all that is holy prompted you to buy the farm?"

"It was my favorite place as a kid. I felt safe and loved there. I had no idea it was being used to stash contraband. You didn't bother to warn me. Not one word from you! Danny is the only one who warned me away, but that was an effort to cover his crimes. Why didn't you tell me?"

"This isn't my fault, young lady. You were never supposed to step foot on that farm again. Uncle Frank assured me that he could keep you away. He absorbed it into his holdings, and we were free to walk away with no strings. Freedom is precious. Then you went and bought the place and landed right in the middle of a huge mess." Her dad folded his arms over his chest and glared at her.

"I just wanted a quiet place to put down roots. When I saw the farm for sale, I had to buy it. I couldn't let it go to someone outside the family. It's a shame you don't understand that, Dad." She trembled in frustration.

"Let's calm down. Everything is resolved now." Tammy patted her shoulder from the back seat. "I understand you were instrumental in bringing more than one person to justice, Sally. I'm proud of you."

"Thanks, Mom. I wish I hadn't stumbled into the whole

thing, but things are good now."

"God has a plan for all of us. You're stronger now than you were before. You're about to be married now where you were completely alone before. It all transpires according to God's plan." Her mom met her gaze in the rearview mirror as she spoke.

"If we had any idea you could possibly be put in danger, we would never have left the country. We would have made certain you were kept safe. We love you." George's voice echoed through the car.

"Sweetheart, we had no idea you even thought about country life. We thought you were happy with your career. You never gave us any indication you wanted anything different." Tammy picked at the seam of her jeans.

"I haven't spoken with you in over three years. How would you know if I've been happy in my career?"

"I'm sorry. I just assumed." Tammy's eyes reddened as she stared out the window.

"Will we be seeing Jake this evening?" Her dad's voice was soft and soothing.

"No. He's staying at his place tonight. He doesn't want to invite bad luck by seeing me before the wedding. He told me we've had more than our share, which is a fact."

"I suppose that's true. I look forward to seeing him tomorrow before the wedding then."

CHAPTER 44

Brilliant purple irises lined the path, ever reaching for the crystal blue sky. Standing guard over the wedding venue, the old farmhouse sported gleaming windows and a fresh coat of sage green paint. Birdsong accompanied Detective Shawn Wilson on a lone violin while over a hundred people sat in cloth-covered folding chairs and waited for the big moment.

Jake and Reverend Tom strode to the altar from the front porch with giant smiles. Detective Wilson played a haunting tune as Chase and Christy met at the end of the path and slowly marched forward arm in arm. Christy's single purple iris complemented her lavender mid-length gown that showed off dark purple western boots. Chase's dark jeans and yellow western shirt lent a festive splash of color. Once they were in place, everyone stood and turned to watch Sally and her father glide up the aisle.

Sally felt radiant in a purple satin dress with lace overlay. The sweetheart neck revealed her something borrowed – Pam's gold locket with Chase's baby picture nestled inside. The tea-length skirt showed off her new white distressed cowhide western boots with purple vine pattern embroidery. Wearing a blue rose in her nut-brown hair, bold purple eye shadow gave her dark brown eyes a smokey look. She carried a silk flower bouquet of purple hydrangeas, white peonies, purple hyacinths, and purple roses held together with a lavender ribbon.

Her heart leapt into her throat as she stepped up to the altar, and her dad took his seat.

Reverend Tom motioned to the crowd. "Please be seated."

The good reverend then launched into the typical wedding pronouncements, but Sally could only hear the beating of her own heart. She managed to respond to the "I do" parts, but her mind was swimming in a sea of love, sudden nerves, and fear of messing things up.

Jake seemed to notice that she wasn't focused on the reverend because he gave her hand a slight tug.

Realizing it was nearly time to recite the vows she'd written, her heart fluttered and her mouth went dry. Handing Christy her bouquet, she struggled to breathe evenly as she placed her hands in Jake's.

"I understand that you have both written some vows you wish to share," Reverend Tom intoned.

Jake's eyes sparkled as he gazed into Sally's. "Sweetness, I promise to always be there for you to hug, kiss, talk to, yell at, and provide a shoulder for your tears. I will hold you when you're scared or cold. I will support you when you take on new adventures and fight beside you when you battle. I will stand with you no matter what comes our way, and my love for you will only grow stronger. I promise to always be yours."

Sally fought the tears that tried to spill down her cheeks. She took a deep breath to steady herself before she spoke. "Jake, I promise to be your voice of reason, your partner in crime, your greatest cheerleader, and your lover for the rest of my life. I will always be there to brighten your day, care for you, and lock horns with you when you're stubborn. I will support you in good times and bad. I will fight beside you, always. I promise to always be yours."

Reverend Tom's eyes glittered with moisture. "We will now symbolize the union of Jake and Sally through the blending sands. Each of these two colors represents Jake and Sally's uniqueness and individuality. They have chosen to blend together their lives as the two colors of sand are now blended together."

Sally picked up a tall glass bottle of purple sand labeled "Hers" while Jake picked up the one filled with yellow sand labeled "His." Together they slowly poured their sand into a heart shaped glass bottle labeled "Ours." The sand was nearly to the top when Sally's hand spasmed. She jerked her bottle, spilling purple sand all over Jake's yellow shirt.

"Oh no!" she cried.

Jake chuckled. "It's okay, Sweetness. Just a little sand."

"What if it's bad luck?" she asked.

His lips lifted into a half grin. "So, what else is new?"

The reverend grinned at their exchange. "As these grains of sand are now inseparable, so too are Jake and Sally's lives."

The reverend asked, "May I have the rings?"

They each reached for their respective rings. Jake fumbled with Sally's and sent it flying through the air.

"I got it," Chase called, leaping for the ring that flew through the air in a high arch. The teen caught it with the finesse of a professional baseball player. He stood and handed it back to Jake.

"I'm sure glad you're here to save my butt, kid," Jake whispered. He held the ring up high so those gathered for the wedding could see that it had indeed been rescued from folly.

After the chuckles quieted, Jake turned back to the

reverend and placed Sally's ring in his hand.

"Jake and Sally's rings are a symbol of the bond of love which unites their two hearts."

Sally got lost in Jake's eyes and missed some of what was said but regained her senses in time to utter the sacred, "With this ring, I thee wed."

Reverend Tom smiled brightly. "As you have pledged yourselves to each other in the holy bonds of marriage, as a minister of Jesus Christ, and by the authority vested in me by the laws of Missouri, I now pronounce you husband and wife. You may seal your vows with a kiss."

Jake slipped his arms around Sally and drew her to him with a gentleness she had never dreamed possible. His lips took hers in a sweet kiss that promised a lifetime of happiness. He pulled away and whispered, "You're mine forever now."

The reverend nodded. "May God add His blessing and keep you to fulfill your covenant from this day forward. Turn and face your family and friends."

They turned and looked out at their loved ones' smiling faces. Some were tear-streaked. Others radiated the joy of the moment.

"It is my great pleasure to introduce to you, for the very first time, Mr. and Mrs. Hill. May the grace and love of God go with you all. Amen."

The crowd erupted in applause. The couple began making their way back down the aisle with Chase and Christy in tow. Everyone was startled by Zeke shouting, "No, Ma!"

CHAPTER 45

All eyes turned to Ma, who held a shiny silver pistol above her head, pointing at the sky.

Her cheeks grew pink under the crowd's scrutiny. "What? Don't you people know a little lead is good luck?"

Zeke stepped close to Ma, easing her arm down. "I think they'll be just fine without any celebratory gunfire. You and I really need to have a chat very soon."

Glaring at the sheriff, Ma slipped the pistol into the pocket of her jeans.

An audible sigh from so many breaths being released at once whispered through the wedding party, and the happy couple made their way to a majestic Hawthorn tree to receive their guests.

One by one everyone filed through the line, sharing hugs and handshakes with the happy couple. When it was Zeke's turn to congratulate Sally, he pulled her close in a tight hug.

He whispered, "Welcome to the family, Sally Sue. We're glad you've chosen to join us. You'll make a fine wolf someday."

Her heart fluttered at his words as she argued with herself about the future.

After everyone had filed through the line, Sally and Jake made their way to the long table set up in front of the house. Their three-tier wedding cake dominated the space. The frosting was white with brown streaks that made it look like a birch tree. The topper was two gray wolves. One wolf wore a top hat on his head and a ribbon around his neck. The other wolf wore a veil on her head, a diamond ring on her left front paw, and a garter belt around her left leg. A heart-shaped sign stood just behind the two wolves who were touching noses proclaiming, "The Hunt is Over."

Christy sidled up beside Sally with a bottle of chilled bubbly for the wedding toast. "The cake is gorgeous! I would never have thought of a birch tree for inspiration."

Sally smiled at her friend. "We chose birch because it represents new beginnings."

Christy nodded, filling the glasses. "I wish you the very best of new beginnings."

"We all deserve them, my friend. Remember that." Sally glanced up in time to catch Detective Wilson staring intently at Christy.

Christy raised her glass for the matron of honor toast, and the crowd fell silent. "I'd like to propose a toast to Jake and Sally. May they bask in their love for each other for the rest of their days. Cheers!"

The wedding guests raised their glasses.

Chase stepped forward and raised his glass of orange punch. "I'd like to propose a toast to Mom and Dad. There's never been another couple who deserved happiness more than them." He faced the happy couple. "Thank you for making us a family."

The guests raised their glasses and shouted their agreement.

After the toasts, Sally took the knife in her hand. Jake

covered her hand with his, and together they cut their wedding cake. Jake took a small piece of cake and gently slipped it past Sally's lips. She took a good size bite, moaning a little as the vanilla flavor burst in her mouth. Then she took a small piece and offered it to Jake. Opening his mouth, he took the whole piece along with her fingers into his mouth. His lips slowly released her fingertips and he swallowed the cake whole.

"All the single ladies need to line up over here," Lizzy, the photographer, called. "Come on, don't be shy."

A dozen or so women crowded around the indicated area. Sally regarded her matron of honor for a moment. "You're single now. Get over there."

"No. I don't need to be thinking about such things. Go ahead and throw your bouquet."

"Not happening until you are over there where you belong with the others, Christy." Her lips set in a stubborn line. "Don't make me mad on my wedding day."

She slumped in defeat. "Okay, Sally. Whatever makes you happy." She tromped over to the anxious bouquet hopefuls.

Sally turned her back and swung her arm. "One, two." At the last moment she turned to face the ladies and yelled, "three!" as she launched the bouquet straight to Christy in a pass that would have made any quarterback proud.

Christy caught the flowers rather than letting them hit her in the chest. Her cheeks flamed as she looked around at the gathered crowd.

"Okay, it's the guys' turn now," Jake announced.

He removed the purple garter from Sally's leg and turned his back on the single men in the group. Detective Shawn Wilson and Chase stood over to the side.

"I think we'll be safe over here," Chase told him.

Jake closed his eyes and flipped the garter. It sailed straight to the detective who looked at it like it was a snake.

"We need a picture of the lucky people who caught the

bouquet and garter," Lizzie called.

She herded Christy and Shawn over by the irises. "Now, scooch together a little closer. You aren't going to give each other cooties. Shawn, put your arm around her. Christy, put your head on his shoulder."

Sally watched in amusement as they followed the instructions, awkwardly posing and smiling. Lizzie took a few shots before telling them, "Thanks! I guess this means you two are next!" She hurried off to take more pictures, leaving Christy and Shawn staring at each other.

Sally stifled a giggle as she watched her friend and the detective try to laugh off Lizzy's words. She had a feeling these two would be seeing a lot more of each other. But for now, she had other things on her mind. She had a honeymoon to enjoy.

ABOUT THE AUTHOR

Margarite Stever grew up in Asbury, a tiny Missouri town of just over 200 people. She lives in a larger city now but tries to stay true to her small town, country roots. She has a Bachelor of Arts Degree in English from Missouri Southern State University.

She writes stories and essays that touch a person's heart. She is a member of Joplin Writers' Guild, Missouri Writers Guild, Sleuths' Ink Mystery Writers, serves on the board of Ozarks Writers League, and is Vice President of Ozarks Romance Authors. She published her short story collection, *Moonbeams and Ashes*, in October of 2021.

Her work has appeared in *Romance, Poetry, Mystery and More: An Anthology by Ozarks Romance Authors Members, Chicken Soup for the Soul: It's Beginning to Look a Lot Like Christmas;* Joplin Writers' Guild Anthology, *Seasons of the Four States; Anthology 2019 Sleuths' Ink Mystery Writers*; *Missouri's Emerging Writers*; *Legends: Passion Pages*; *50-Word Stories* website; the 2021, 2019, 2018, 2017, and 2016 issues of *The Crowder Quill;* the Fall 2015 issue of *The Maine Review; Mamalode Magazine's 2015 Better Together;* and *Writer's Digest 2014 Show Us Your Shorts Collection.*

You can visit her website at www.margaritestever.com. Her seeds of wisdom and joy can be seen on her blog at http://ozarksmaven.com/, which has been read in over 90 countries.